Ellie Dwyer's Startling Discovery

Diane Winger

DEDICATION

To all those who devote time to help others – thank you
for your caring, your commitment, and your service.

To Charlie

Not all those who wander are lost.
There's nobody I'd rather wander with than you,
but let's not repeat the "lost" part.

ACKNOWLEDGMENTS

It's amazing how even a few carefully-worded tweaks can bring a scene to life and strengthen the impact of the overall message. I'm ever thankful for the input from my friend and editor, Val Burnell, for helping me enhance my writing and improve my storytelling ability.

Charlie, my husband and muse (can a muse be male?), once again supplied the spark that inspired this book. After realizing he had lost his camera while tackling a highly technical, off-trail excursion to climb the Vishnu Temple formation within the Grand Canyon, he decided to return to the area to search for it the following year. Remarkably, he located the camera, although it was no longer functional. The photos on its memory card contained no surprises, of course.

As always, Christine Savoie created a delightful cover, and I'm thankful for her consistently excellent design work.

Thanks also to Howard Paul of the Alpine Rescue Team and to Tricia Eischied of the Ouray Rescue Team and Ouray Mountain Sports for their patience in answering my many off-the-wall questions about what happens during a search and rescue operation. If anything I wrote about SAR teams seems a bit "off," the error is mine. While I'm at it, here's a huge shout-out to all the incredible volunteers with organizations like these.

Finally, the support and encouragement of my readers has been tremendously gratifying. Together, I feel like we've all come to know and love Ellie and Ruth, creating a delightful circle of friends (real and imaginary) who may never meet in person. Thank you for sharing my fictional world!

Chapter 1

What was that?

I pause, then maneuver slowly backward along the trail, my eyes focused on the slope above me. There! Something is reflecting the sunlight, like a flash bulb that blinds me for an instant. I need only tilt my head slightly to avoid its brilliance, although I still see an afterimage floating in my field of vision.

Curious about what might be up there, I take a cautious step on the loose dirt above the trail. It immediately collapses under my weight, and I stagger awkwardly to regain my balance.

"Ellie! Are you all right, dear?" Ruth has caught up with me after stopping briefly to tighten the lace on her hiking boot. "What were you looking at?"

"I'm fine," I say, stomping my shoe on the ground to knock off the dirt that just covered it. "There's something metal or glass up there, I think. Something shiny, anyway. But the ground is too soft here to climb up to it."

She tries to spot the reflection, but apparently she's too short to see what I did. "How far up is it?" she asks.

I point about six or seven feet above the trail.

"I'll give it a try. Just give me directions as I go." With that, she moves ahead on the trail about twenty feet and starts making her way diagonally up toward the shiny object.

"Almost there. Another step or two. There, about hip level." I shake my head in amazement. Ruth is so petite and moves with a grace I'll never achieve. Who would believe this tiny lady will turn 85 in a few months? She's my inspiration, my best friend, and my favorite camping companion. Even with nearly twenty years difference in our ages, I still find it hard to keep up with her.

"Got it!" she says, digging something out from the wild grasses, small rocks, and mossy loam. She brushes it off, blowing to remove more dirt. "It's a camera." She holds it up in display for a moment before beginning her descent back to the trail. A few tiny rocks roll as she steps back the way she came, while I imagine the minor landslide I'd probably cause if I tried to follow that same path.

"What an odd place to find a camera," I say as she hands it to me to examine. Much of the camera is encrusted with crud, yet the rear display screen is streaked and partially clear of dirt. That must be what reflected the sunlight.

"Maybe, with all the heavy rains they had around here last weekend, it washed down from somewhere above us. You saw how soft the ground was where you first tried to climb up."

"I'll go with that explanation. *Soft ground* sounds a lot better than *clumsy woman*."

She chuckles. "Oh, Ellie. You don't give yourself enough credit."

Not expecting anything to happen, I try pressing the camera's on/off button. Nothing. I locate the door to the battery compartment and manage to slide it open after removing more crud using my fingernail. "Ugh. The batteries are all corroded."

"I wouldn't expect it to still work, even with good batteries," Ruth says. "But we should take it with us anyway. Leave no trace, and all that."

She has me stick it inside a pouch on the outside of her

pack. "Even if it's damaged beyond repair," I say as we resume our hike, "I wonder if the memory card is readable. Wouldn't it be cool if we could figure out who it belongs to and get the photos back to them?"

"It would indeed! But, how do we read the memory card if the camera won't function?"

I know we can take it to some business that offers photo printing services. But we're camped for just two more nights in a remote campground in the Sangre de Cristo mountains of southern Colorado. The nearest town that might be useful would be a few hours away. Perhaps we can find something when we hit the road with our two camper-trailers to meet up with Ruth's daughter at Skylight RV Campground closer to the Denver area.

Another idea hits me. "Ruth, don't you still have a little point-and-shoot camera?"

"I believe so. I haven't used it for a while, since my phone takes such nice photos. Why do you ask?"

"Maybe we can read the memory card from this broken camera in yours." I feel like a kid who can't wait to open a present. I'm not sure why, but I'm feeling quite excited about viewing the pictures and solving the mystery of whose camera this is.

I try to focus on the scenery around us rather than obsess about the hidden treasure we've dug up. The southern mountains of Colorado offer lovely views and varied terrain of tall, snow-capped peaks in July bordering one side of a valley, while rounded, densely forested mountains outline the other. As our trail climbs, we emerge from a dense copse of Aspens and Ponderosa pines into a broad meadow covered with an explosion of wildflowers. Rugged cliffs rise dramatically from the edge of the expanse. We both pull out our phones to capture the spectacle with our cameras, which makes me start thinking about my earlier discovery again. The trail did eventually loop back above where we found the lost camera, so perhaps someone dropped it while hiking and forces of nature toppled it down a hundred feet or more over time. Has it been out in the elements for a year? I'm guessing longer. How many people still use point-and-shoot cameras? Has it been five years? I have no idea.

Ruth announces that she needs to "use the facilities," which in this case means finding a private spot off the trail. Not that we've seen many other people today, but it's almost a guarantee that a party will come along the moment one of us drops her drawers. She side-steps downhill to crouch behind some trees. Personally, I'd rather look for a flatter location.

"Just don't fall over and tumble down the slope," I call out to her as I retrieve a packet of shelled sunflower seeds from my pack. I can't help but imagine myself in that exact predicament. It isn't a pretty picture, which is why I'll wait until I find an easier spot. Meanwhile, I struggle to tear open the cellophane wrapper protecting my snack. After pulling and clawing and clamping it between my teeth, I take a breather, trying to recall where my little pocket knife is stowed in my pack. Ruth rejoins me just as I start wrestling with the package again.

"Would you like me to give it a try?" she asks.

Why not? Naturally, she gets the cellophane to tear open immediately. Handing it over, she says, "You probably had it ready to rip open. It just needed one more try."

Good, because I really didn't feel like searching for my knife anyway. We continue along the trail as I decide the opening in my sunflower packet is slightly too small. In an instant, the cellophane rips along the complete length of the container, sending an arc of seeds flying through the air and cascading down into the vegetation along the side of the trail. With a sigh, I note that about a dozen tiny seeds remain in the corner of the package, so I tap them into my mouth, hoping the local birds and chipmunks enjoy the feast I've left for them.

We arrive at our destination – a small but lovely alpine lake, unnamed on our map. Perched on a massive, flat boulder, we both dig out our lunches from our backpacks.

"I'm so excited to see Carol and Nick in just two more days!" Ruth says, her face lit up with an enormous smile. Carol Goldman is her oldest of two daughters, and takes after her mother. She loves being outdoors, especially hiking, and is as high-energy as Ruth. We've met up with her and her husband a number of times to visit National Parks, although the pandemic caused us to postpone and re-think some of our plans over the past two years. I love Carol's company, although it sometimes feels odd to realize that she's barely younger than I am, yet my closest friend is her *mother*. Nick tends to be somewhat quieter and laid-back, which fits as a good balance to Carol's high energy. Both are very intelligent, warm people who I enjoy greatly.

"And then I'm off to spend time with *my* daughter and her family," I add. "You know, Ruth, you're still welcome to come with me to Denver to visit them."

She reaches over and squeezes my arm. "It's not that I don't want to meet them in person, but you need time together to continue building your bond. I'm so happy that you've connected with your biological family. Looking back on how things worked back when you were a teenager, it seems unfair that you and your daughter were kept in the dark because of sealed adoption records."

"That might still be the best for some situations. Still, I'm very happy that things have worked out the way they have for us. Maybe I should have been making more of an effort to see them other than on video calls these past couple of years, but that's been complicated recently. Besides," I say, breaking my chocolate bar in half and handing off the rest to Ruth, "I still feel like I need to let her set the pace, so to speak, of our relationship. I don't want her to feel like I'm trying to take the place of the parents who raised her."

This is a conversation Ruth and I have had many times. As usual, she reassures me and reminds me to simply be direct with my daughter in asking what she wants or does not want from our relationship. As if it were that easy.

Ruth purses her lips, looking slightly embarrassed. "Remind me again of their nicknames. Is your daughter Cagney or Lacey?"

I chuckle. "She's Lacey. Her best friend in middle school went by Cagney."

She smiles, "And they were obsessed with the show about two take-control, women detectives."

"Yep. Cagney and Lacey was like a female 'buddy film' about a decade before Thelma and Louise."

"With a happier outcome. And your granddaughter goes by Em. That's easier, since it's just a shortened version of her name."

"Right. I'm still working on remembering to call them by their nicknames, since they clearly felt it was a special deal to share them with me. Anyway," I say, licking my lips to remove any errant chocolate, "this coming week we'll focus on enjoying being with Carol and Nick. I assume you and Carol have already planned out a ton of hikes for us."

She laughs. "Don't worry. We've included some rest days in the itinerary. Well, at least one rest day."

I moan, but can't suppress my grin. This is how vacations with the mother-daughter superwomen team always go. I'll be worn out, but it'll be fun.

Chapter 2

Back at the campground, Ruth and I huddle at the table in her camper as I perform surgery on the camera. I extract two batteries that look like they've been coated in salt. "Yuck," I say as I deposit them in a small bag to be disposed of later. After cleaning the battery compartment as best I can with the eraser on the end of a pencil, I insert new batteries.

"Here goes," I say, pressing the power button on top of the camera.

We're both astonished when the unit hums and the lens starts to emerge. A split second later, we hear a crunching, scraping sound as the mechanism grinds to a stop.

"That didn't sound good," Ruth says. "Do you think we can clean it off so it can open all the way?"

I examine the partially-extended lens and shake my head. "I think the dirt is inside. Let me try again." I press the power button a second time, and the poor thing emits an even uglier sound as it tries to retract back into the body of the camera. It shudders, then freezes. Giving it one more shot, we hear only a faint click as the camera dies completely.

"Okay. On to Plan B," I say, opening the access slot and pulling out the SD memory card.

We make progress using Ruth's old point-and-shoot

camera to accept the found camera's card. After confirming that we're seeing unfamiliar photos using her little Canon's viewing screen, I connect it to Ruth's laptop and start the transfer process to its hard drive.

"This may take a little while," I say as I look closely at the progress bar display. "But I think somewhere within these 832 photos, we'll find some clues to work with to figure out who lost their camera."

"Over eight hundred shots? Do I have enough room on my computer to store all those?"

"I think you'll be fine. I'm going to go fetch a memory stick from my camper and make a copy so we can both scan through them whenever we've got some down time." I glance at the cat, who has been sitting beside Ruth, watching our entire operation closely. She's eyeing Ruth's original SD card and I see her reaching a paw toward it in slow motion, probably hoping nobody will notice. "No, Charli, that's not for you," I say, snatching it before it gets swept off the table. Or chewed on. She mews at me, swishing her tail in annoyance, jumps off the bench seat, and retreats to a sunny spot by a window.

"Small, bright things are irresistible," Ruth comments.

"The two of you think alike," I say with a smile, noting Ruth's customary brilliantly-colored outfit, her sparkly earrings, and her newest addition, a tinsel-like effect in a stripe on her short gray hair.

By the time I return, the transfer is complete. I copy all the photos to the backup device and we begin scrolling through the shots, starting with the most recent.

"Look," she says. "That's the same meadow we saw with all the wildflowers. I recognize the mountains in the background."

"They must have been there later in the year. The snow's all gone from the peaks."

We click on more images, looking for shots of people. There are a few showing someone hiking ahead of the photographer, possibly a man with a yellow backpack and a green ball cap, his back to the camera.

"Here he is again," Ruth notes. This time we can see a bit of his face in profile. He's sporting a light brown goatee and has a strong jaw-line and straight nose. He's standing on a broad rock, feet spread wide and arms akimbo, his pack on the ground beside him. "I remember that spot," she says. "Oh, and look at those arms. He must pump iron, don't you think?"

I nod in agreement. He's what I would describe as "husky." Not fat, but I could imagine him becoming overweight if he doesn't keep up his exercise regimen now that he's approaching middle age. Maybe he played football in his earlier years.

The next photo shows him from farther away, in the same macho stance, and the scenery he's facing is gorgeous. The sky is like a canvas of intense blue, shot through with streams of white mare's tail clouds, indicating winds high above.

As we continue our inspection of the pictures, moving backwards in time, we observe scenes that may be around the photographer's home. Blooms in a garden; cut flowers in a vase on a kitchen counter; monkeys and tigers and giraffes in a zoo; pink flowering fruit trees; a wintry scene of pines, their branches hanging low under the weight of heavy snow. Now and then, we spot a person at a distance, probably unaware of the camera.

Our journey through time takes us through the brilliant colors of autumn and to an image of a baseball field. "The Colorado Rockies," I say, noting the predominance of purple clothing in the stands and recognizing the peaks in the distance. They were the backdrop of my childhood, growing up in Denver.

The images move back to a series of somewhat blurry shots taken at night of a fireworks display above a distant mountain in silhouette. I recognize it as well – Pikes Peak, but from a different perspective than I'm used to. Next, there's a summer gathering with a number of different people, streamers of red, white, and blue decorating a long table covered with dishes of food. "I think this is the hiker man again," I say, pointing to a guy with a goatee.

"I think so, too," Ruth says. "And there he is with that 'Superman' stance like he had on the overlook."

We both giggle.

"But who is taking the pictures?" I say, flipping through the assortment more quickly, in search of more face shots. There's Superman again, with his yellow backpack. Neither of us recognizes the scenery, although we agree that it may be in Colorado.

Finally we locate a posed photo of Superman and a woman, his arm around her shoulder. Could she be our mystery photographer? She's friendly-looking, with a broad, warm smile. Long, straight dark hair, a golden-brown complexion, and huge, brown eyes. "Lois Lane?" I ask.

"Could be. She seems a lot happier about having their photo taken than Superman does. Is that a forced smile, or what?"

"It looks more like a grimace than a smile. Maybe someone slipped him some kryptonite."

We study the photo for a minute before Ruth asks, "Okay. We think we've found the owners of the camera. Now, how do we actually get in touch with them?"

After a long pause, I reply, "I have no idea."

We stare at each other, waiting for the other to come up with a proposal. Ruth shrugs. I raise my eyebrows and gesture with one hand, palm up, as if an answer might be conjured that way.

"The boys!" we say in unison.

Of course! To us, "the boys" means none other than Ruth's grandson Gabe, and his partner Ethan. Or, I should say, his *husband*, since the two of them tied the knot early this year. Although Ruth has four grandsons in all, somehow only Gabe and Ethan have become "the boys" to us. Ruth won't admit this out loud to anyone in her family, but there's no doubt in my mind that these two are her favorites. Mine, too. We've shared some delightful adventures together.

Ethan is a computer guru of some sort who helped me out of a tight spot a few years ago with his high-tech abilities. Gabe manages a hotel and seems to do a lot of "social media" stuff to connect with customers so they'll choose to come back to that property and recommend it to friends. "I'll bet they can come up with a plan to make the story of this camera 'go viral'," I say, offering an enthusiastic *thumbs up.*

She mirrors the gesture. "Let's give them a call right now."

***

"Grams!"

"Ellie is here too, Gabe, on speakerphone."

"Grandma Sorta!" he exclaims. That's their cute nickname for me, because he and Ethan consider me to be *sorta* another grandmother. I chuckle as Ethan shouts from the background, "Hi Grams! Hi *Gramasoda!*" It's that delightful New England accent of his.

We tell them about our interesting find and our theory that we've discovered photos of the people who owned the camera, or at least a close friend. "We still have about 400 more pictures to review, so maybe we'll find even more clues," I explain. "But surely somebody will recognize the guy. Even if the woman isn't the photographer, Superman will certainly know who is."

Upon my mention of our *Superman* nickname, they ask to see at least one image of the man. "I'll send you a couple of shots of him plus the one where he and a lady are posing. If we find others that show their faces, or any other clues about their location, I'll get those to you as well."

"The files may have the exact locations as part of their metadata," Gabe says.

Ruth and I exchange puzzled looks. "What's a metadata?" I ask.

"No worries, *Gramasoda*. Metadata is just some information stored along with the photos. But I'm not sure it'll apply here. What you described sounds like an inexpensive, older digital camera, so it may not have had GPS capabilities, in which case the coordinates couldn't have been saved with the photo."

Ruth leans closer to the phone. "In English, please."

Gabe answers, "That camera is probably too stupid to know where it was at. In other words, you can just forget about the last minute of this conversation."

We all get a chuckle out of that.

"I think I'll set up a special email address where people can respond if they have information about the photos. I should probably just screen the messages first, then send any on to you that seem legit."

"Thank you, Ethan," Ruth says.

His comment makes me realize that we may receive all sorts of oddball responses. I'm relieved that he'll sort through them before we see any. I shudder, thinking of the potential spam, fake come-ons, and possibly porn that a "viral post" might generate. He's a brave man.

They sound excited about the project, with ideas pouring out of them for ways to reach a large audience. Much of the jargon goes over our heads, but that doesn't matter.

"Okay, Grammas. We're on it!" Gabe declares as we sign

off from the call.

Ruth and I both let out a long breath in unison. "That was exciting," she says.

"Very." I stand and stretch tall, stiff from sitting hunched over the phone.

"I'll send them the snapshots we picked out. I wonder how long it will take for someone to respond?"

"Could be right away. Could be never. I guess we'll just have to wait and see."

Ruth wraps me in her arms in an exuberant hug. "I feel like we're in an Agatha Christie story!"

"Or an episode of Cagney and Lacey."

Chapter 3

"Charli, wanna go for a hike?"

Ruth has set their new kitty backpack on the floor, open and ready for Charli to hop inside. The cat stares at her, tilting her head to one side. "She knows 'wanna go outside'," Ruth whispers, "but we're still working on 'wanna go for a hike'."

I wave a feathered toy on a stick and wiggle it inside the pack, where the moving feathers can still be seen through the mesh back panel. That does the trick. Charli makes a swift leap into the carrier through the open side panel, attacking the make-believe bird. After a moment or two, she loses interest in that and pops her head out, meowing.

Ruth scratches the cat's head. "Ready to be picked up? Here we go."

With just a little bit of help from me, Ruth lifts the backpack up and shoulders the straps. Charlie climbs out and drapes herself across Ruth's shoulders, one of her favorite places to ride and get a different perspective on the world.

Laughing, I pick her up and stuff her back inside the carrier. "Not this time, Charli. We're going on an actual hike and you get to ride along." This time she settles in, peering out at me as I zip up the mesh door.

When I first met Ruth, I was surprised that she let her cat

explore outside without being on a leash, but soon observed that Charli never ventured far from wherever Ruth might be. I learned that she is only allowed to roam once they've stayed at a campground for at least three or four days, giving Ruth time to scope out any potential hazards for the cat, and giving Charli time to feel settled in. Recently, Ruth got the idea of taking the kitty along on some short hikes. She's managed to convince Charli that a harness and leash aren't the end of the world, but it hasn't exactly been a joyous experience for either of them. This kitty backpack idea is still in the experimental stage, but so far Charli seems almost as happy to be inside the pack as she is whenever presented with a cardboard box or a paper bag. Well, maybe not quite *that* happy, but I'm setting the bar extremely high with those comparisons.

Yesterday, we managed to walk around the campground loop and she did well with that. Now we've driven both of our campers to Skylight RV Campground, located about ninety minutes southwest of Denver, where we'll be staying for this coming week. Carol and Nick have just arrived as well, and we're all going to head out to hike the short nature trail that starts right from the campground.

A knock comes at the door. "Mom! It's us. Are you guys about ready?"

"Coming!"

We join Ruth's daughter and son-in-law outside, where they make a fuss over Charli in her new carrier. Carol unzips one of the mesh openings and scratches the cat's head, rewarded with loud purring. "What a cute carrier! She seems so comfortable with it. Does she get restless after a while?"

Ruth shrugs. "We don't really know yet. This is only her second outing, and the first one was only about ten minutes."

"One of the cool things about this pack, though, is that there's a mesh 'tunnel' we can fold out when we stop, so she can move around more and still see all around her," I say.

"Cool. Well, let's see how she does." Carol sets off toward the start of the nature trail, and we all follow her lead.

"So, Ellie," Nick says, matching my stride. "I understand you'll be starting to get Social Security next year. I'm turning 62 soon, and thinking of taking it early. Why are you waiting until you turn 66?"

Interesting. Nick and I usually talk about travel and favorite books and his hobby as an amateur astronomy photographer. I wouldn't have expected retirement income as the first topic out of his mouth. Not feeling completely comfortable with discussing details of my financial situation, I simply say that I felt I could get by until my full retirement age and want to lock in the higher earnings at that point. As soon as I can manage it, I try to distract him from the topic. "What does this say?" I ask, hurrying over to an informational sign along the path and quickly skimming the first paragraph. "Oh, that's interesting. Did you know that trappers and fur traders traveled through this area?"

Either Nick takes the hint, or he finds the information on the sign fascinating. He stands and studies it carefully. Meanwhile, Ruth and Carol – and Charli, of course – have continued walking and are quite a distance ahead of us. I decide it would be impolite of me to try to catch up with them, leaving Nick behind, so I wait for him to conclude his perusal of the reading material. After a bit, he looks up and seems to realize that I've been waiting for him.

"Sorry," he says. "I guess I got a bit lost in thought there." He chuckles awkwardly. "I'm really not that slow a reader."

I smile, hoping to put him at ease. "No problem. I imagine it takes a little while to decompress from work and all that driving you guys have done these past couple of days. Ruth and I have the big advantage of being on permanent vacation. We're always decompressed."

He nods, his smile looking far more natural. "We're definitely ready for a break from work and everything. I'll try to turn off my hyper brain and move into relaxation mode."

I let out a little snort. "If you can call a week planned by the mother-daughter energy team 'relaxation'. Have you been able to get any details out of Carol on what they have in store for us? Ruth just keeps saying, 'trust me.'"

He doesn't say anything for a moment. I glance over at him, and his eyes are fixed on the smooth path ahead of us. Distracted by his thoughts again, I imagine. When he notices me looking his way, he manages to mutter, "Yeah," but I'm not sure he even heard what I was saying.

We hike on in silence. Looking ahead, I see that the ladies have stopped, and Carol is helping her mother remove the cat backpack and setting it on the ground. Ruth notices us and waves. As we draw closer, I see that they've pulled out the extension tunnel from the pack and Charli is lying inside, her head swinging this way and that, checking out the world around her safe little cubby. So far, the kitty carrier seems to be a success.

"You two must be getting into some pretty deep discussions. I know you can both hike much faster than that," Ruth says with a wink.

"Just checking out all the signs," Nick says.

Ruth grins at her daughter. "We've been so busy catching up that we haven't been paying any attention at all to the stops along the trail. What have we missed? Anything really special?"

Since it doesn't seem like Nick plans to answer that question, I mutter something about traders and trappers. "A lot of it has been things we're already familiar with, like information about flora and fauna, climate, things like that. But still interesting," I add, not wanting it to sound like I hadn't really been reading the signs. Even though I had barely skimmed most of them.

"So, Mom and I have picked out a hike for tomorrow. It's about a thirty-minute drive from camp to the trailhead, and there's a good trail. If I remember correctly, it's about nine miles round-trip and there should be some great views at the top." Carol sounds quite excited about their choice. She and her mother are both smiling ear-to-ear and I swear Carol is actually bouncing on her heels.

"So, how high will we be climbing to get to 'the top'?" I ask.

Ruth answers, "I believe the summit is close to 12,000 feet." Seeing the look on my face, she adds, "But the trailhead starts at over 9,000 feet, so we'll only be climbing around 3,000 feet."

Yipes – that's crazy! She and I spend a great deal of time camping in Arizona at elevations under 3,000 feet. These past several days, we made it to Colorado and have camped at 6,000, hiking as high as 8,000 feet. This will be a big jump. I hope our bodies have acclimatized enough that we won't have trouble with the altitude. And poor Nick and Carol! They just drove from the California coast over the past two days.

Although a hike like that would have been utterly impossible for me several years ago, I remind myself that I'm in far better condition now that I'm a full-time camper and frequent hiker. If we were planning on hiking nine miles with 3,000 feet of elevation gain in southern Arizona, where our highest point might be lower than we'll be starting out tomorrow, I'd say I could probably manage it, although it would challenge my stamina.

I inch closer to Nick to whisper in his ear. "If it gets to be too much for us, you and I can always turn around early."

He nods, then whispers back, "At least there's one other sane person in our group."

Carol squats down to pet the cat, but looks over her shoulder at us. "We can still hear you guys, you know."

***

This evening, after visiting with the Goldmans around a campfire in their camp site, Ruth and I excuse ourselves around 9:00, figuring we'll all need an early start for our long hike tomorrow. Walking back to our own campers, I bring up what's been on my mind much of the day.

"Does something about how Nick is acting seem 'off' to you?"

Ruth pauses, glancing back over her shoulder to make sure no one is within earshot. "Carol confided in me that they've been having some problems lately. She didn't go into any details, so I really don't know any more than that. Nick seems like his body is here but his brain is somewhere else."

"That's a good way of putting it. On our other trips, I've found him easy to talk to. Today, it was like pulling teeth to get him to say a word."

We say our goodnights and I return to my cozy little A-frame camper, where I lay out hiking clothes and ready my backpack for the Long March tomorrow. Plenty of energy bars and snacks, extra water, and a will to live. I remind myself that I sometimes surprise myself by achieving more than I think I am capable of. I also remind myself that I can always turn around early if it truly becomes too much for me.

Maybe Nick will open up to me about what's troubling him. There's no doubt in my mind that Carol and her mother will have plenty of time to talk while zooming up the trail far ahead of us mere mortals.

Before settling into my bed, I take a few minutes to scan more of the photos from the mystery camera. I don't find anything particularly useful, although it dawns on me that Lois Lane and Superman seem to only have gone on two hikes that were recorded on this memory card, although the timeline seems to include at least two years of changing seasons. Lois – assuming our guess that the photographer

20

really was the woman Superman posed with – seemed mainly interested in taking photos of museum exhibits, food, rainbows, snow on a back porch, fireworks, and Christmas decorations.

Enough screen time – I've got to get some sleep.

Chapter 4

There's a chill in the air when we climb out of Ruth's truck at the trailhead. Although sunrise was almost two hours ago, this deep mountain valley hasn't been touched yet by its warming rays. I slip into an extra jacket over my two layers of clothing, draw on a warm hat and lightweight gloves, and tighten my boots. I'm sure I'll be down to a short-sleeved shirt in a few hours, but I have plenty of room in my pack to carry them.

"Everybody ready?" Carol says. She and Ruth high-five each other, I signal a thumbs-up, and Nick simply nods. "Let's do it!"

Ruth and her daughter take off like a pair of horses out of the racing gates. Nick and I trudge behind. "Slow down, you two. My muscles need a few minutes to warm up," I call out, and they oblige.

"So, Nick," I say, settling into a comfortable pace, "have you been taking photos of any cool constellations or galaxies or whatnot lately? I haven't seen anything from you for a while."

"Nah. I haven't been using my telescope much lately. It seems like there's always so much going on, or we don't have clear skies, or ... I don't know. I just haven't felt the urge."

I'm shocked. He upgraded some of his equipment a couple of years ago, even building a small observatory in their back yard. Astronomy was his passion. What could have happened to change that? Is he depressed? Is that part of what's going on with him and Carol?

I wait a while before trying another topic. "I've come across several novels recently that were based on the idea that there are an infinite number of parallel universes. Apparently, that's an actual idea among scientists studying quantum mechanics or string theory, or something like that." I chuckle, "As if I have any idea what those really mean. Anyway, I'm sure the novels are oversimplifying the concepts. Still, I find the idea fascinating. Have you read anything along that line?"

"Yeah. Multiverses. Every time there's a 'choice' that we make – 'we' being people, plants, air molecules, cells, or anything else – the universe splits into versions where each possible choice was made. Very interesting to think about. What books have you read that you'd recommend?"

Bingo! There's the Nick I remember. We enjoy a lively discussion of readings, both fiction and non-fiction, speculate on how time travel stories might be woven into parallel universe tales, and Nick even jokes about Charli and Schrodinger's cat. "When she's in her new carrier, she's both awake and asleep until someone observes her."

We catch up to Ruth and Carol, who have stopped to remove outer layers of clothing, now that we've climbed to a portion of the trail that is in the sun. "What are you two laughing about?" Ruth asks.

"In *this* universe," I say with a smile as I take off my pack, "we're laughing, but in another universe we've just killed Schrodinger's cat and we're pretty upset with ourselves."

"O...kay—" Ruth says, drawing out the syllables. Carol rolls her eyes. "How's everybody doing? Is the pace better?" Ruth asks.

"Don't worry about us," Nick says. "We're not that far behind, right?"

"Not at all. You're doing fine. We'll stop regularly and let you catch up and take a break if you need to. We've got all day."

Nick focuses on Carol and smiles. She reaches out a hand and he takes it, giving it a squeeze. "Be sure to drink enough," she says quietly to him, looking at him with more tenderness than I've noticed since we all got together.

He nods. "I'm good." Turning toward me and Ruth, he adds, "She's always looking out for me."

Good. Maybe whatever disagreement they've been having is over with. I hope so.

The mood feels relaxed as we take off again up the trail. I pair up with Carol for a while so we can chat, but as we gain elevation, I'm finding it more difficult to speak in more than short phrases at a time. She's doing remarkably well with her breathing, considering how little time she's spent at this altitude. We've pulled ahead of Nick and Ruth, and I'm relieved to stop to catch my breath. After they catch up to us and we take a short break, we revert to our previous configuration of the fast ladies leading the way while Nick and I set an easier pace. I'm able to walk and talk at the same time again.

We've climbed above the dense forests to an elevation where the trees have become more sparse. The scenery has opened up, presenting us with a spectacular cirque ahead. The rugged mountains are arranged like an enormous amphitheater with our trail approaching the open side of the partial circle. Stripes of snow delineate north-facing drainages, and we skirt past the final, tenacious clusters of trees as we climb above tree line. We pause, and my eyes follow the snaking line of our trail ahead as it curves around to a steep slope on the right side of the cirque, then follows it upward toward a towering summit.

"Doing okay?" Carol asks as we take another break.

"Are we heading way up there?" I ask, pointing to the highest point ahead of us.

"That's it. We've got about another 1,000 feet to gain and maybe a mile in distance. Are you guys good with that?"

I'm getting tired. I try to assess how I'll feel in another hour or so of steady climbing up what appears to be a steeper trail than what we've experienced so far, and then imagine how much energy I'll have reversing the entire path. "I think this is far enough for me. I'm fine waiting here while you go up the rest of the way."

"Same here," Nick says, much to my relief.

Ruth and Carol both nod. "Good. I wouldn't want to leave just one of you back here alone," Ruth says.

Carol adds, "We'll go on ahead, then. If you want, head back down to that last cluster of trees. That looked like a good spot to relax, and if the wind comes up, you'll have a bit of shelter."

"Are you sure you don't mind waiting?" Ruth asks. "We'll probably be at least ninety minutes before we get back to you."

"Not a problem," Nick says as I nod in agreement.

"We're fine," I say. "Have fun and be careful."

We stand and watch them move away at a swift pace, then turn around and ease our way back to the meeting spot Carol suggested. Our conversation turns to theories about the people who lost their camera.

"Where do you suppose they dropped the camera?" he asks. "Was there a trail up above where you found it?"

"That's been a puzzle for us," I say, shading my eyes as I peer out at the distant peaks. "The trail did eventually wind back around above us, but that camera had to tumble about a hundred feet downhill to get to where I spotted it, which seems odd given all the trees and bushes and rocks on that slope. The only idea we've come up with is that the heavy rains in the area last week washed it down."

"I guess that could be. Any idea how long it had been out in the elements?"

"Actually, your son and Ethan figured that out after we sent them some of the photos. What did they call it?" I pause, trying to remember the term. "Oh, yeah – metadata."

"Oh, sure. The date would be stored as part of the metadata in the photo files, so you can tell exactly when each one was taken."

Am I the only one who didn't already know what *metadata* is? "Right. The final picture in the camera was taken just under three years ago, and the dates go back another two years or so beyond that."

"And what was in the final photo?"

"The last three were of Superman at an overlook. None of them really showed his face well, so we didn't have Gabe and Ethan post them online."

"Do you think Lois Lane set the camera down after taking those shots and then forgot it?"

"No, the overlook wasn't above where we found the camera. Not even close. I guess they must have hiked back down a ways and somehow lost the camera later. Maybe it fell out of a pocket. It's too bad that neither of them noticed it."

We sit in silence for a bit, contemplating the mystery.

"Well, you've certainly got the right team for spreading the word about those photos. I'll bet the boys will figure something out."

"I'm optimistic."

"Maybe those people were abducted by aliens, and the camera was dropped from a spacecraft."

I laugh. "Maybe the camera is a portal to another

universe. If only we could clean all the grit out of it, we could try it out."

He nods at me, a serious look on his face. "In another version of our universe, you are Lois Lane and you've forgotten that you ever lost your camera."

"Or you are Superman, who, by the way, is from another planet, and *you* are the one who abducted these people and discarded the camera."

"I think the altitude is getting to us. Maybe we need to focus on breathing until the ladies return."

***

After a dinner of campfire stew, prepared by Nick and Carol, Ruth and I excuse ourselves early and walk back toward our own campsites. When we arrive at her camper, she gestures for me to come inside with her, but holds a finger to her lips. Wondering why we are trying to be silent, I follow her up the steps and move quietly through the door.

She points toward the couch where I spot the kitty backpack, its "tunnel" expanded. Inside, Charli suddenly notices us, lifting her head and vocalizing a greeting.

"You left her in there all this time?"

Ruth chuckles. "It's more like she's refused to come out all this time. When I fed her before going over for dinner, she took a few quick bites and hurried back to her new favorite perch." The cat, now bright-eyed and alert, moves into the main backpack compartment, sticks her head out the top opening, and starts mewing at us.

Ruth shakes her head at the cat. "No, Charli, we're not going for another hike right now. I need to get my regular pack ready for tomorrow, but then I'll take you out for a little bit." Remarkably, she quiets down and crawls back into the extension.

"Stick around for a few minutes if you don't mind, dear."

Ruth's voice has turned serious.

"Of course I don't mind."

She sighs, gesturing for me to sit in her comfortable easy chair, her usual favorite spot. "That's okay," I say, sitting at the end of the couch where I can reach inside the cat carrier to massage Charli's cheek. "We're fine here."

"I had a long talk with my daughter today," she begins. "Of course, I wouldn't share our conversation with just anyone, but she said it would be fine if I talk to you. She knows how close we are."

I lean forward, wondering what could be coming next. I'm very fond of Carol, thinking of her as being like a sister. She's let me know that she feels the same about me. "What's going on?"

Ruth runs her hands along her thighs, as if smoothing the fabric of her hiking pants. "I don't know if you've noticed, but things are a bit tense between the two of them."

I nod. "Nick finally loosened up late in the day, but he's seemed distant. I hadn't really noticed Carol acting differently, but of course you know her so much better."

"She says they've been quarreling about money, which has never been a problem between them in the past, at least to my knowledge. As you know, Nick's mother died this past year. The funeral and burial costs were considerable. His father died about twenty years ago, and apparently they had a life insurance policy on him that covered the expenses, but there was no policy on his mother. Nick wanted to take out policies on himself and Carol so neither would be burdened financially if the other died, but Carol didn't think it was necessary, since they have plenty of money in savings and investments.

"Were they able to come to any sort of compromise?" I ask.

"That's the problem, at least from Carol's perspective. She thought the matter was still undecided, but Nick went out and bought two costly, high-coverage life insurance policies without telling her. She only found out when she was checking to see if they had received a credit on their bank account for something she had returned for a refund. They had quite an argument about his secrecy on top of overriding her opinion before they could come to an agreement."

Ruth's face is drawn and her voice is filled with her distress. Charli emerges from her new favorite cozy place and leaps up on Ruth's lap, peering up into her face intently. "Hello, little one," she says, stroking the cat's head. "It's all right. I'm going to be fine."

I shake my head, imagining how upset I would have been if Franklin had ever made a decision to spend a significant amount of money on something when he knew I was opposed to the purchase. That wasn't how we did things in our household. "Where do things stand now? Have they come to any understanding?"

She rocks a hand side to side. "On the surface, yes. But neither one is happy with the so-called *compromise*. Carol insisted that they cancel his policy, saying she was certain she could manage the expenses if he dies before her. In turn, Nick insisted on keeping her insured. Carol is willing to go along with that if he'll reduce the coverage to something she considers reasonable, like $25,000."

Thinking back, I remember dealing with my husband's funeral. Franklin was cremated, which I know is less expensive than burial, but that cost considerably less than $25,000. "That sounds reasonable. How much, if I may ask, is he insuring her for?"

I gasp when she reports that Carol's life is insured for half a million dollars. "And he's saying he just wants to cover funeral expenses? That doesn't make any sense. It's not like she has decades of future income that they want to protect. They're both planning on retiring within the next five years, right?"

Nodding, Ruth agrees. "Exactly the arguments Carol has

been making. But he's dug in his heels and she's having a hard time accepting that they're paying a hefty premium so he won't have to dig deeply into savings should she die first."

I sit back and consider the situation. "Maybe he just needs some more time. It hasn't been terribly long since his mother passed away, and this may be part of his grieving process. I understand why Carol would be upset, but do you think she'd be willing to put this on the back burner for, say, six months and see how they both feel by then?"

Ruth smiles and nods slowly. "That seems like a wise suggestion, dear. If you don't mind, I'll talk to her about your idea next time we get a chance to be alone together."

"Which is probably during tomorrow's hike," I say, grinning. "I don't mind at all. I think it's better coming from you." I rise from the couch. "I should probably get everything ready for tomorrow. You said it would be easier than today's hike?"

"I think it will. We'll be hiking up to a lake that's lower than today's summit. Only 2,000 feet of elevation gain and seven miles round-trip."

I start my internal Little Engine mantra: *I think I can, I think I can.* That's still near the upper limits of my stamina, but at least there's a *possibility* I can manage tomorrow's entire hike.

Before I leave, I help Ruth hoist the cat in her carrier up onto her back. "I'm going to have to learn to put this thing on without help, but if Charli doesn't mind a few moments of twisting and turning, maybe that's not a problem," she says.

They accompany me to my camper, then continue their outing. As they depart, I can hear Ruth talking to the cat, who responds with a variety of vocalizations as if they are deep in conversation.

Minutes later, as I finish filling up my water bottles for tomorrow's hike, I hear voices outside my trailer. They sound like they are right beside my door. I pull back a curtain and am surprised to see a man and woman setting down a bundle of firewood and a bunch of camp chairs beside the metal fire pit in my campsite. I swing the door open, but before I can speak, the woman says, "Hi there! We didn't think anyone was home. You don't mind if we build a fire, do you?"

Is she serious? They want to have a fire in *my* campsite? And hang around for a few hours? What's wrong with their own site?

"Uh, actually yes, I do mind. You understand that that fire ring is in my site, number 19, right?"

They exchange glances, appearing to be quite puzzled by what I've said. "But this is such a nice spot," the man says, as if that might change my mind. "There isn't nearly as much room for all of us where we're staying."

All of us? How many people are we talking about here? "No. I'm sorry, but I've paid for this spot and I don't want a group of strangers coming in and taking over my site. You'll have to make do with the site *you've* paid for."

The woman huffs, but starts gathering up the chairs. After scowling in my direction, the man retrieves the bundle of firewood and the two depart.

That was weird. For all I know, they aren't even staying at this campground.

Weird and creepy.

Chapter 5

Ruth and I checked the weather forecast early this morning and recommended that we all throw an extra warm layer in our packs, *just in case*. "They're calling for possible snow showers at higher elevations today in the afternoon," I say as we gather at my site, prepared to load up my Nissan Xterra with our packs.

"That can't be right. Snow showers?" Nick says, sounding incredulous. "It's the middle of July, for heaven's sake."

Having grown up in Denver, I know it's quite possible. Today's high in Denver is predicted to be in the mid-90s. Up at 10,000 feet elevation, we're expecting a high of 55, but thunderstorms often build up in the mountains later in the day. Today, that storm may bring snow instead of rain.

"Don't worry," I say. "The forecast is for less than an inch of snow up high. We may be back to the car before it even begins."

I sound pretty darn sure of myself, don't I? That's because I've been repeating *I think I can* in my mind ever since we saw the forecast. I've hidden my initial panic quite well, I'm pleased to say.

Once the Goldmans have retrieved warmer fleece sweaters to wear under their raincoats, should they be needed, everyone climbs into my SUV and we drive to the trailhead.

The sky is an amazing shade of deep blue, without a cloud to be seen. As we experienced yesterday, there are short stretches of trail within thick forest that remain muddy and sloppy from earlier rains and even the last patches of winter snow finally melting. We're able to skirt around the messy sections, often following the tracks of hikers that preceded us. When we emerge into sunnier areas, the trail is dry and wildflowers are in bloom. The air is crisp and cool, but as we progress up the path, we all decide to stop for a minute to shed a layer of clothing or swap out a jacket for something lighter.

"I'm actually sweating," Carol says, stuffing her coat into her pack. "Doesn't that sun feel wonderful!"

I scan the sky, noting the first appearance of a few fluffy, white clouds. "So far, so good on the weather," I report.

Nick crouches low to take a photo of the wildflowers with his phone. "This is gorgeous. I still can't believe it could snow up here."

"It might not at this elevation, but once we climb another thousand feet, it's more likely," I explain. "Or maybe it won't snow at all. The weather forecast doesn't change the actual weather."

"That's for sure," Ruth says. "Is everybody ready to continue? There's a lake waiting for us up ahead."

"Onward and upward!" Carol says, and takes off at a swift pace. Her mother accepts the challenge, and although both Nick and I start hiking as well, the two of them pull well ahead in no time.

"That's probably the last we'll see of them until we reach the lake," he says.

I smile and shake my head. "But look at them. They're having such a blast. I can't even imagine what they were like when Carol was growing up."

He grins. "Oh, I've heard stories. You know, Carol was

totally her mom's kid, always ready to take on any challenge or adventure. Climbing trees, jumping off high places – that didn't always end well. Taking up rock climbing. Signing up to learn to skydive! Valerie had more of their dad's temperament, fun-loving but ... not *cautious* so much as—" He pauses, searching for the right word.

"Sane?" I suggest.

Laughing, he comes back with, "Well, there's that. But I was going to say *balanced*. Or *practical*. If it weren't for David and Valerie's more stable influence, those two would have gotten into a lot more trouble than they did."

"Still, I wouldn't want Ruth to be any other way. I think her exuberance is what keeps her young."

"Yeah." He's silent for a dozen paces. "Same with Carol. I wouldn't want her to be any other way, either. Still, I sometimes worry about her. I just want her to be safe. That's not unreasonable, right?"

Is this his signal that he might want to talk about what they've been quarreling about? He probably assumes that Carol has talked to her mother about the insurance business, and he may be probing to find out if I've been in on the conversation. I decide to tread carefully. "We always hope the people we care about will be safe. With Ruth, I try to find a balance between wanting her to be okay and knowing that adventure and excitement are part of who she is."

After a minute or so goes by without him responding to my comment, I figure that Nick isn't going to say anything more. I focus on the scenery, glancing up from the trail frequently at the rugged skyline to our right, spotting a waterfall in the distance that must be a few hundred feet tall. I'm about to point it out to him when I hear him say, "Uh oh."

I stop and turn around to see what he's reacting to. He's stopped about twenty feet away, looking back and toward the left of our trail. Although the sun is still shining down on us where we stand, to the west I see black. A mass of dark clouds hovers in the distance, a curtain of gray and white hanging beneath them.

"Uh oh," I concur. "I think that's our snow showers."

Rats. My instinct is to turn around immediately, but what about Ruth and Carol? Should we try to hurry and catch up with them so we can all stay together? Or will they notice the weather moving in and turn around on their own?

"What should we do?" Nick asks. I'm sure the same thoughts are going through his mind.

"I don't know," I say, looking up the trail, where the sky is a mixture of blue sky and innocent-looking puffy clouds, then back at the storm approaching. I unclip my backpack and set it on the ground. "For the moment, I'm putting on more layers," I say, hurrying to pull clothing from my pack. He follows my lead.

The wind is picking up and I can feel the temperature dropping. By the time we've donned our packs again, there's a light mixture of rain and soft, mushy snow or sleet pattering on the hood of my raincoat. "I think we need to head down," I say.

"But what about Carol and Mom?"

His voice is filled with stress. "Nick, listen. I'm worried about them, too. But who in our group are the most experienced hikers? Not the two of us, right?"

"Right," he says with a deep sigh.

"Right. I think we need to head down just a short way where the trees are thicker. That'll shelter us a bit. Maybe this will pass through quickly. Then, if they haven't shown up yet, we can head back up the trail to check up on them. Are you okay with that?"

The wind pushes my hood off and I cover my head again with it, pulling the drawstrings tighter and turning my back to the wind.

"Okay. That makes sense," he says, ducking his head against the storm. It's totally snowing now, flakes sailing in an almost-horizontal path. "Let's go!"

We scurry down the trail, which is rapidly turning white. So far it's not slippery, but I stay alert to that possibility any moment, using my trekking poles to improve my chances of staying upright if the surface does turn muddy or slushy. With the noise of the wind, I can't tell if Nick is right behind me or not, and a quick glance over my shoulder offers me no more information, since my hood blocks most of my peripheral vision.

"I'm right behind you," he shouts, probably having noticed that I slowed down to try to look around.

"Just ahead!" I yell back, spotting a copse of tall evergreens where I hope we'll find some shelter from the wind and snow.

Once there, we push aside wet, dripping limbs, ducking and weaving so we can huddle close to the trunk of a mature ponderosa pine. We sit on our packs, side-by-side, leaning back against the red-mottled bark. The surrounding trees and bushes have cut the wind to just a slight breeze, although all the branches are swaying and moving around us. "I smell vanilla," Nick says.

I breathe deeply "Mmm. That's from the tree."

We sit in silence, our view hemmed in by the protective grove of trees.

"Is that my imagination, or do you hear music?" I ask.

He listens. "Can you believe it? They're singing in the blizzard."

Sure enough, I can make it out now. *Let it snow, let it snow, let it snow!*

We crawl out of our hidey-hole and spot the ladies hiking swiftly down the trail toward us, singing exuberantly. Ruth spots us first and waves a pole in the air. "It's snowing!" she announces.

"We noticed."

The left side of her jacket is plastered solid with snow. The right side is clear. Carol's looks the same.

"I think it's almost over," Carol says, gesturing back toward the clearing. Indeed, it doesn't seem as dark as before, and the wind has died down to almost nothing. The snowflakes have become larger and seem to be floating in place.

"Come look at the meadow," Ruth says, having retraced her steps.

We follow her to the open terrain and gasp in awe. What had been a green blanket surrounding a field of colorful flowers is now even more spectacular. It is now a tapestry of small clumps of white offsetting the blues and reds and yellows of the partially-covered blooms. "Definitely another photo opportunity!" Nick says, framing shot after shot of the beauty surrounding us. The tops of the peaks around us are hidden in misty clouds, which are swirling and dissipating before our eyes. I pull out my phone as well to take photos, as we all *ooo* and *ahh* as the sun makes an appearance for a moment, then is hidden by clouds again. The snow has ended.

"Since everything is wet and another squall might move through, I suggest we head back down," Carol says. "Unless anybody really wants to try for the lake?"

We all shake our heads, although Ruth seemed to wait until she had already seen how Nick and I were voting before she agreed. After spinning slowly a full 360° to take in the views one final time, I follow the others back into the woods and down toward the trailhead.

Once at the car, we shake out our rain gear and spread the damp coats on top of our packs in the back of the vehicle. Ruth and I brought along dry shoes to change into and a garbage bag to hold our sloppy footwear, but Carol and Nick just do their best to scrape off excess mud and ride back to camp wearing dirty, damp boots. "Sorry for the mess," Carol says.

"No worries. The rubber mats are easy to rinse off."

I start to walk around to the driver's side to get in when I hear Nick whisper loudly at his wife, "See? Today was a perfect example of how something could happen to one of us."

"Don't start!" she answers. I pretend I didn't hear the exchange.

All three of them doze off during the drive back. I fend off my own drowsiness with special chewing gum that offers a generous shot of caffeine, something I carry in the car for just this type of situation. I get the boost without having to stop every fifteen minutes to pee, as I would if I drank a large cup of coffee instead.

Everyone is awake again when I turn into the campground and pull up to my site. My mouth drops open.

"Who are those people?" Carol asks. "Was something messed up with your campsite reservation?"

I recognize two of the strangers gathered around an enormous blaze surging from the fire ring in my site. They're the couple from last night.

"I can't believe they came back," I say, quickly relating the story of how I already denied them permission to use my spot.

Ruth huffs. "I'm going to tell them to leave immediately!"

"Hang on a minute, Mom," Nick says. "First off, I'm not sure they'll listen to a tiny, eighty-five-year-old lady."

"I'm still eighty-four. Don't rush it."

"Sorry. Still, there are a lot of them. And I see a lot of beer bottles. I think we need to ask the camp managers to deal with this. If they don't feel like they can control the situation themselves, at least they have the authority to call the police if it comes to that."

We all stare silently at the intruders. If any of them has noticed us, they've made no move to leave or to even come over to the car to talk. I back up and drive to the campground office.

"Hi! What can I do for you folks?" The woman behind the counter is wearing a sizable name tag reading "Neva Joyce Fischer, Manager." Perfect.

I smile, "Hi, Neva."

"Neva Joyce," she responds, smiling warmly.

"Neva Joyce," I repeat. My three companions, who all felt the need to accompany me into the office, pipe in with a chorus of *Hi, Neva Joyce*. We're a friendly little group.

"I'm having a bit of a problem at my site," I say, noting that my team members are nodding in agreement. I explain what's going on as Neva Joyce's eyes widen and she nods, acknowledging her agreement that I shouldn't be required to host a bonfire party against my wishes.

"I'm so sorry that's happened. Tell you what," she says, picking up a walkie-talkie. "Is there another site you can go hang out at for a little bit?" She scans our group of nodding heads as my three friends all answer *Sure* and *Of course*. "Good. Jerry or I will come find you once we've got things straightened out at your site. Can you give us about twenty minutes or so?"

"Absolutely. Thank you so much, Neva Joyce. I've never had anything like this happen before, so I wasn't sure what to do."

She clicks on the radio. "Jerry?" It squawks back with an indecipherable reply. "Pick up Arnold and meet me at site 19 in five minutes. We have some rowdies. Over." Another squawk. She nods and smiles our way. "You did the right thing coming to us instead of trying to deal with that group yourselves. We'll take care of it."

It's closer to an hour before a man wearing a long-sleeved

polo shirt with the camp logo drives up in a golf cart to Carol and Nick's site where we're all sitting around the picnic table, munching on snacks that they've set out. "We're all set," he says. "This was the second time somebody's complained about those folks. Most of them weren't even registered to be here. They've packed up and left. We've doused the fire, but would appreciate it if you'd stir the ashes and smother any hot spots you might still find."

"Thank you so much!" I say, with my gang all repeating variations on that theme.

What a relief.

Once the campground employee putters away, Carol says, "I'll understand if you say no, but what do you all think of us building a fire and roasting some sausages for dinner? I can cook them inside if you'd prefer."

"Fire!" Ruth says, raising her hand.

Nick does the same.

I laugh. "It's unanimous. Fire!"

I'm confident they'll build one that's sufficient for cooking, but not a blaze that stands taller than I am.

Chapter 6

"Look at that!" Carol says, her face pressed against the car window. "It's like a storybook castle!"

I'm our designated driver again, since Ruth's truck isn't that comfortable for four people, while Nick and Carol came out here in a rented camper van. I've always wanted to see Bishop's Castle for myself, having known about it for years through magazine and online articles. I pull off the two-lane highway, finding a spot in a line of parked vehicles. I've barely caught a glimpse of the building, since it is surrounded by dense forest, but when I exit my car, I spot what appears to be a metal dragon's head poking out through the high treetops.

We find the entrance and walk a short distance to the base of the incredible building. My eyes follow the stone and metal structure up and up and up, until I find myself leaning backwards to try to take in the summit of the castle. Arches and towers, airy metal walkways with frightfully delicate-looking handrails, windows and arrow slits and ramparts and other features I've seen in fantasy illustrations but can't name, soar at least a hundred feet into the air.

"No moat?" Ruth asks, stepping into an entry hall where signs tell us to sign in to a registry and that serves as a release of liability at the castle. There are hand-painted signs everywhere. The builder of the castle, Mr. Bishop, is clearly not a big fan of rules, such as building codes, but he declares the structure as being a work of art which doesn't have to comply with such restrictions. And an incredible work of art it is.

Nick points at a curved walkway high above us. "What's holding that in place? We need to stay off of those things. One slip, and you'll be gone."

Carol sighs deeply. "What's happened to your sense of adventure?"

"Adventure?" he says. "Hey, I'm fine with exploring the parts that look like they'll hold up. I mean, all the rock work looks as solid as can be. But those railings! Look at that spiral staircase leading up to the metal bridge between the towers. One false step..."

"I know," Carol interrupts. "So we'll be extra careful, and if you don't want to climb up there, nobody is going to try to convince you to try."

"Come on, dear," Ruth says, taking her daughter by the hand and practically dragging her toward a stone staircase. "I want to explore."

Nick huffs in frustration as they disappear into the darkness of the entrance. "They'll watch out for each other," I offer. "It's worked for them for sixty years, right?"

Nick stares at the entrance, still shaking his head. "I suppose."

"Let's go inside," I say, leading the way. The place is just as incredible inside as out. There are dark spiral staircases offering narrow views of the outside world as we climb. We emerge into a gigantic room suitable for a gala ball, the ceiling soaring up to a sky lit apex far above us. I spot Ruth and Carol traversing the building on one of the outside catwalks that looked so precarious from the ground. They seem more substantial up close, but are definitely not for anyone with a fear of heights. Out another window, I grin as

I discover a close-up view of a metal dragon head arching over the forest below. A story I read about this place explained that the dragon was designed to spew smoke and fire, but after a few demonstrations of its remarkable design, Mr. Bishop was ordered to stop firing it up before he burned down the surrounding forest. I'll have to content myself with viewing photos of the phenomenon rather than witness a fire-breathing dragon in person.

I look around for a doorway to access the outer walkways, and realize that Nick is no longer in sight. Feeling brave and curious, I follow another woman through a passageway and find myself at a similar outside pathway. I step onto the crisscrossed metal surface cautiously, avoiding looking straight down between my feet, and grasp the handrail. Taking a few steps at a time, and focusing straight ahead, I start to relax and take a moment to look out over the treetops at the surrounding mountains and hills. When I hear a child shouting, "Mom! Look at me! Look at me!" I make the mistake of looking down at the people milling about on the ground far below. Yipes, those people look like ants!

I follow the path as it circles the side of the building, looking for the next opening where I can retreat to the security of the indoor space. Before I reach it, I hear Ruth calling, "Ellie! Up here!"

Grasping the railing with both hands, I look up and my breath catches in my throat. Far above me, on the flimsy-looking bridge that spans between the castle's towers, are Carol and Ruth, smiling and waving. With both hands.

"Hold on to the railing!" I shout back. I can't believe they aren't hanging on. You couldn't pay me enough to get me to step out on that thing, much less let go. If you forced me up there, you'd have to pry my hands loose to bring me down again.

They move to the end of the bridge and I let out a sigh of

45

relief. That is, until I spot them climbing up to an even higher perch inside a sort of metal geodesic dome at the very summit of the structure. I can't bear to watch, so I duck inside the building and try to focus on the incredible detail work that Mr. Bishop put into creating walls and arches of stone. This fantastic creation of his has taken decades of single-handed labor and passion and a unique vision. It's just that I prefer being up close and personal around his rock and concrete work rather than his metal walkways, which I'd rather admire from a distance.

I explore, looking for passages that lead downward, back to the good old ground. When I emerge into daylight, I scan the building, looking for my companions. Nick appears by my side. "I think they just went back inside," he says. He doesn't sound happy.

We both freeze when we hear a blood-curdling scream. "Oh my god," I gasp. "Did someone fall?"

Looking around frantically, I try to determine where the cry came from and what has happened. I spot a woman pointing up toward the dragon head, then the person beside her is craning her neck and thrusts her arm upward, pointing as well. Shading my eyes, I peer upward, searching for what they've spotted.

A woman's voice from high above us screams, "Save me!"

There she is! A woman dressed in a purple gown and a matching tall, pointed hat with a veil is standing on a high walkway just below the dragon's head. She gestures dramatically, placing the back of a hand on her forehead. "Save me!" she shouts again. "The dragon is holding me captive."

A new character appears on a steep outside staircase spanning two stories that climbs toward her position. He's dressed as a knight, literally in shining armor which catches the sun and leaves me with spots before my eyes. Although I'm no longer terrified that someone has fallen, I'm now fretting over the fact that he isn't holding onto the railing, since his sword and shield are occupying both hands. Earlier, I considered climbing those stairs, but only took four steps before retreating. As I said, it is frighteningly steep and narrow.

"What a relief," Nick says as we watch the hero lay down his sword and sweep the kidnapped princess into his arms. "I thought something terrible had happened when she first screamed."

"So did I." My stress level has fallen slightly, now that they are both on the horizontal pathway, although I'd still like to see them holding onto something besides each other.

With the show apparently over, Nick and I explore the grounds and walk through the on-site gift shop while we wait for our companions to descend. We spot the performers posing for photos in front of the castle. The knight has set aside his props, and is standing with hands on his hips, feet spread wide, trying to look serious and noble. There's that Superman pose again.

Once Carol and Ruth show up, we drop a donation in the box near the entrance, and head back to my car. Ruth is bubbling with excitement, unable to wait until we get back to camp to show me some of the photos she's taken on her phone. They watched the big rescue from a high perch above the dragon head, and had spotted the costumed woman before she screamed.

Carol has grown silent after she and Nick spoke quietly to each other on the walk out. I couldn't hear their conversation, but it's easy to guess the topic. I can't get used to how different they're behaving on this trip than any of the other times we've been together. They're usually both so upbeat, enjoying our activities as well as enjoying each other. Maybe I'll ask Ruth if they've ever been like this in the past.

I suppose I shouldn't be so surprised. Thinking back on my marriage to Franklin, we had many wonderful times, but there were rough spots now and then. And obviously, I can't just write off that time he left me. That makes what Carol and Nick are going through seem like nothing at all. I should just try to stay positive around them and hope that helps jog them out of their funk enough so we can all enjoy ourselves this week. I'm sure they'll work things out.

Back at camp, Ruth and her daughter invite me to go for a walk around the grounds with the cat along on her new leash. I decline, wanting to do more sleuthing in regard to the mystery camera.

When Ruth first tried Charli out with a regular collar, kitty wanted nothing to do with it. The moment she felt the slightest tug on her neck, she flopped down on her side and refused to move. Ruth would pick her up and try to set her on her feet, but Charli would simply go limp and lie down again, looking up at Ruth with the most pathetic expression imaginable. But once Ruth switched her to a tiny body harness that didn't put any pressure on her throat, she's accepted the idea. Most of the time. Today she seems content to explore with her new contraption on, and hasn't resumed licking it furiously as she did the first time she wore it.

I boot up my laptop and click on one of the better shots of Superman. Ethan emailed me this morning, reporting that they haven't received any useful responses to the posts about the camera on social media. "What about non-useful responses?" I asked. "You don't want to know," he responded. He's probably correct.

He described an interesting thing I could try on my own, explaining that it could be quite time-consuming but might help identify either Lois Lane or Superman. Of course, I know how to search online based on words and phrases, but Ethan gave me a link that lets me upload a photograph and do a search for similar pictures. Although he didn't have any immediate success with the shots I sent over to him and Gabe, I'm hoping I'll find other pictures of this couple if I can devote more time to the effort.

After about an hour of scrolling through images and trying out multiple shots of people, all I've learned is that both men and women may strike that "super hero" pose that our target has adopted. The search returned pictures of Marilyn Monroe, a Rembrandt painting of an Admiral, Wonder Woman, Santa Claus, toned athletes, cartoon characters, toddlers, and a plethora of average-looking men and women, standing with arms akimbo. I may be the only person on the planet who has never been photographed in that pose.

I'm calling this a dead end.

Chapter 7

While the trails we visited earlier this week were obviously not well-known, that isn't the case today. Instead of seeing only one or two other parties in a hour's time, I feel like we're hiking with a cast of thousands. Despite setting out quite early, there were already a dozen cars in the large, paved parking lot by the trailhead. I'm sure the lot is filled to overflowing by now.

Fortunately, almost everyone is still moving in the same direction – uphill. Two young women, obviously in excellent condition, passed us soon after we started out and have just passed us again on their way down. "Do you think they went all the way to the third lake?" I ask my companions.

Ruth pauses and turns to watch them sprint down the trail. "At that pace, it seems possible."

Nick gazes at the two fit runners until he notices Carol frowning at him.

"I wouldn't be surprised if they go climb two or three other mountains today, while they're at it." Ruth is beaming in delight, her eyes sparkling as she's probably imagining what that would feel like, having that much stamina.

Carol nods in agreement. "Even when I was running track in college, I don't think I could have kept up with those two. I'll bet they run ultras."

"Ultras?" I ask.

"Ultra-marathons. Those are races that are even longer than marathons, so more than twenty-six miles. I know there are several ultras in Colorado. Like the Leadville 100 and the Hardrock 100."

"One hundred as in *miles*?" I ask. She nods. "How many days do those take? Do people sleep at a camp that's been set up for them, or what?"

"From what I've read, many of the runners don't sleep at all, while some might take a quick nap. I think the officials make people drop out if they're moving too slowly to finish the race in 30 hours or something like that."

"That hurts just to think about." I suppose if people are capable of doing something that incredible, I can manage to keep hiking one more hour and see all three lakes.

As the trail winds through an open, grassy area, we're able to enjoy excellent views of a long band of tall granite walls a few hundred feet to our right. Nick pauses when he comes to a narrow path taking off from the main trail toward the cliffs. Pointing toward the rock face, he says, "How about that – see the rock climber about halfway up?"

It takes me a moment to spot a figure in an orange shirt stepping up high and gracefully advancing up the wall. "I hope he's using a rope!" I say, thinking about the documentary Ruth and I watched recently about a climber who often foregoes any safety gear, even when ascending hundreds and hundreds of feet off the ground.

"Let's go closer so we can find out," Ruth says, already marching down the secondary trail leading to the rock formations, Carol right on her heels.

I look at Nick. He shrugs, then gestures *after you*. I shrug back, then follow after the ladies, glancing up at the climber now and then as we draw closer. Not 'he' – the climber is a woman, long black hair draping down her back. And she does have a rope dangling beneath her. Not that I understand how a rope below her will help her if she falls. Ruth talked me into going to a climbing gym one time, where the rope was tied to our harnesses from above, so we would just dangle if we fell off. *That* I understood.

We catch up to Carol and Ruth at the base of the rocky cliff, where they are talking quietly to a shirtless, barefoot young man wearing a harness. There is also a woman standing close by, clearly focused on the climber above and gradually feeding a rope through a contraption attached to her harness as the climber moves upward. What's that called again? *Belaying*. I recall that the doohickey on her harness is called a *belay device* and she is the *belayer*. See, my memory still works!

"This is Matthew and that's Sammi," Ruth says in a low voice, indicating the two people on the ground. "And the girl up there is Morgan."

I tilt my head back as far as my neck will allow. Morgan is terribly high above us. "I'm at the crux," she shouts, "Watch me!"

"I've got you," Sammi yells back as she shifts her stance slightly, looking like she is bracing herself for something to happen. I hold my breath. How can Sammi do anything to help if Morgan slips?

We watch as the climber moves her left foot up to an impossibly high position. I've never been that flexible in my life. She rotates her body so her left hip is against the wall, reaches up with one hand, then starts to move upward. "Aaa!" she shouts as she peels off the rock, flying through the air.

"Aaa!" I echo, my hands clutching my chest.

Suddenly, her fall is arrested. After a rapid adjustment of her body position, now she's hanging from the rope a short distance below where she fell. Her feet are propped against the wall, as she dangles in a nearly seated position, looking back up at the spot she called "the crux." She's shaking out her hands as if she'd just washed them and doesn't have a towel to dry them. "Almost had it," she calls down to us.

"Nice catch," Matthew says to the belayer.

"No problem." Sammi looks relaxed now, effortlessly holding the rope taut as Morgan rests above us.

After a short break, Morgan announces, "I'm moving up," and Sammi shifts her position again. "I'm going to put in another piece," Morgan says as she arrives just below the difficult spot.

Watching her actions, and with Matthew's help in understanding what's going on, I learn that the *leader* – that would be Morgan – inserts special pieces of gear into cracks in the rock to act as *protection*. She then runs the rope through a carabiner – a spring-loaded metal loop. With one end of the rope tied to her, the other being managed by Sammi, and something attached to the rock to hold the rope, the system is designed to prevent her from falling very far if she does happen to fall.

"Does that system always work?" I ask.

Matthew holds a finger against his lips, reminding me to speak softly. "Usually," he whispers.

That wasn't as reassuring as I would have liked.

Fortunately, Morgan moves smoothly through the troublesome section and climbs steadily to a stopping point. After a short period where nobody seems to be doing anything, she calls out, "Off belay," and Sammi comes back with "Belay is off. Great job, Morgan!"

I locate a suitable-sized rock and sit down, feeling breathless. Watching this has taken more out of me than any hike would.

"She's setting up a top rope," Sammi says. "Would any of you like to give it a try? There's an easier line just to the left of what Morgan did."

Three voices come back with *No, that's okay* and *Thanks,*

anyway, but – no surprise – Ruth announces that she would love to give it a shot. "I've been to some indoor climbing walls, but I've always wanted to try climbing outside on real rock."

Morgan arrives back to earth, having rappelled down the rope. Her stature is close to Ruth's, and they quickly discover that they have the same teeny, tiny shoe size. It only takes a few minutes for Ruth to don Morgan's harness and shoes and to tie into one end of the dangling rope.

None of us older folks are the least bit surprised as Ruth does a stellar job of climbing up the easier route that the girls pointed out. All three climbers call out words of encouragement and suggestions for technique when she pauses, but she reaches the top without a single slip, then earns compliments as she positions herself properly to be lowered smoothly back to the ground.

"Anyone else?" Sammi offers. We decline, Carol explaining that we'd probably better be on our way if we want to reach the uppermost lake before heading back down to the car.

As Ruth changes back into her hiking boots, Sammi steps close to me and quietly asks me how old my friend is. When I tell her, her eyes open wide. "Guys!" she says at a normal volume. "You'll never believe this! Ruth is older than my grandma!"

"Seriously?"

Ruth is beaming. She loves shattering people's stereotypes about what someone her age is capable of.

Morgan gives her a serious look. "You're my hero. I want to be like you when I grow up."

Ruth pats her on the arm. "Just keep thinking that way, dear, and you very well may do it. Stay active, hold on to your enthusiasm, and don't think you shouldn't do something you enjoy just because you've reached a particular age."

Carol adds, "I hear friends say 'I'm too old to do that anymore' when they turn sixty or sixty-five. That's nonsense. Now, I recognize that injuries and health issues could make it impossible to hike or climb, but I say: *try* to do it before giving up. If you try and fail, that's one thing. If you won't even try because someone told you that you shouldn't, that's a shame."

Like mother, like daughter.

As we resume our hike up toward the lakes, our moods are upbeat, despite the larger numbers of other hikers heading up and down the trail. I'm pleased to listen to Carol and Nick talking about rock climbing outings they've enjoyed in the past, and even toying with planning a trip in the near future to Joshua Tree National Park to give it another shot. "Mom, you and Ellie should join us! We'll find some easier climbs to do and there's also lots of great hiking there. Maybe we could try for next spring."

"We'll look at the calendar when we get back to camp tonight," Ruth says. "Do you think Gabe and Dustin might be able to join us? I'd love to see both my grandsons."

"That would be great if they can get the time off," Carol says. "We used to take the kids climbing when they were young. Gabe was a natural, afraid of nothing. You remember how he was always climbing everything in sight – even when he was a toddler, he would try to scramble up onto the back of a chair, or find a way up onto the kitchen counter. We had to watch him every minute. Dustin was far more cautious on the rock, but if he saw his big brother doing something, he always had to give it a shot. I don't know if Ethan has ever climbed, but he's usually ready to try out new experiences."

Speaking of Gabe and Ethan, I wonder if they've received any emails as a result of the photos they've posted for me. I'll get in touch with them once we're back at the campground where I'll have a WiFi signal. As usual, my phone doesn't have any connection here along the trail.

We reach the first of the three lakes after only twenty minutes of hiking. I don't take any photos, since the shoreline is filled with other people. Children are throwing rocks into the water, two dogs are splashing around, there's a boom box playing something with a bass beat that is making my teeth vibrate, and the overall effect is the exact opposite of what I hope for on a hike.

"I'd say let's skip the other lakes," Nick says.

Carol nods, "I agree. This is a zoo."

With no argument from Ruth or myself, we retrace our path down the trail, often stepping aside for uphill traffic. Where did all these people come from?

Back at the car, we all sigh in relief as I negotiate my way out of the overflowing parking lot. Two vehicles jockey for my spot and I leave them to it. There are cars parked along both shoulders of the highway for what seems like a mile.

"That's it," Carol says. "I had another popular trail in mind for tomorrow, but scratch that. I'll go through my notes and try to find something more obscure. Maybe I'll need to choose something with a crappy road, but if so, we can go in mom's truck if you don't want to take the Xterra, Ellie. I can drive us."

I'm not wild about the "crappy road" idea, but it does have the benefit of keeping the number of hikers down. Crowds on hikes seem to start picking up on Thursdays each week.

She continues, "The good news is that Friday's hike should be a reasonably quiet one, so hopefully we can end the trip on a high note."

"Does it have a crappy road too?" I ask, wondering why it might be a quiet destination so close to the weekend.

"Just a dirt road," she says, "but they described it as being in good condition and not very long. I only found one site online that mentioned it – a blogger who seems to seek out places that aren't well known. But it sounds like it has pretty views of a narrow canyon and cool cliff bands."

That sounds appealing.

Chapter 8

Crappy road doesn't begin to describe the torturous ribbon of rocks and ruts and muddy puddles that jabbed and jostled Ruth's truck as we inched our way toward the start of our next hike. *This will keep the crowds down,* I say to myself, afraid to attempt to speak the words aloud because I'd be in danger of biting off my tongue. *Bam, thunk, thud, wham.* Everyone holds on to anything we can reach to try to avoid bouncing our heads on the roof of the truck cab.

"Sorry," Nick mutters for about the hundredth time as a wheel drops into a particularly deep pit and we all moan and gasp. We know it's not his fault. I consider suggesting we walk the rest of the way instead, since I'm sure we can hike faster than the truck is progressing, but I can't imagine where we could pull off to park. We can only hope that there's a place to turn around once we reach the trailhead.

After what feels like an eternity, we arrive at a wide spot where two or possibly three trucks might be able to park. A shot-up sign indicates that we've arrived at the Bottom Dollar Mine Trail. Glancing at my watch, I'm surprised to note that it's only been forty minutes since we started up the horrible part of the road. Only? Any longer and I think all my teeth would have fallen out. And to think, we've traveled just over one mile!

"Are there any special features we'll be seeing along this

trail?" I ask Carol, who suggested this alternate plan for today. "Lakes? Great views?"

"It's supposed to lead to an old mine," she says. "Hopefully, there'll be some interesting equipment and maybe remains of a mining town, although I couldn't find any details online."

"I've heard that it's dangerous to explore abandoned mines," I say, noting the look of alarm on Nick's face.

Ruth nods. "Definitely. If we find the opening to a mine, we'll keep our distance, right?" She nods at her daughter, raising her eyebrows until she gets an affirmative response from her.

Good. The two of them are always up for adventures, but thankfully they also possess common sense. Usually.

The trail is rocky and uneven, requiring that I keep my focus on where I step. Taking quick peeks around me between steps, I realize that I'm not missing anything as far as scenic views – the forest is dense here. After a while, we come to a drainage which is nearly void of any vegetation. The gravelly surface is a peculiar orange color and we make our way with some difficulty down to the yellow trickle of liquid, our shoes skidding on the rough, sloped surface

"I don't think we want to get any of that on our boots," Ruth says, leaping across the two-foot-wide contaminated water. "They might disintegrate."

"Or glow in the dark," I add. We all follow her example, then battle our way up the matching slope on the other side of the drainage.

Unbelievably, the trail gets worse on the other side. It's rockier, overgrown, difficult to locate, and blocked in places by rocks and boulders, some almost hip-high.

"Are we sure we're still on the trail?" Nick says. "This doesn't seem like we're heading toward an old mine or mining camp."

"It doesn't seem like we're heading for anywhere people

have been before," I add.

We stop and turn slowly in circles, considering our surroundings. "I wonder if the mine was actually straight up that drainage," Ruth says. "We certainly found the mine tailings on its slopes and the contaminated water might have been coming from some portion of the mining operations."

Nobody says anything for a minute. I'm dreading skidding down that sloping, orange wasteland again, but doubt there's a better way to return to the known trail. "You know what?" I say, acknowledging in my own mind what a lousy time I'm having, "I'd like to head back to the car. What are you guys thinking of doing?"

Nick appears relieved. "I'm with you, Ellie."

Ruth and Carol exchange a quick look and mutual nods. "I don't think it gets any better," Carol says. "Sorry about that, everyone. I guess I picked a loser today."

As we retreat, we reassure her that she's not to blame for today's disappointing outing. "We asked for something that gets us away from the crowds, and this certainly measured up to that goal," Ruth says, chuckling.

I manage a sliding tumble down the ugly drainage slope, narrowly avoiding stepping into the nasty water as I regain my balance. Nick holds my hand as I step across, just in case I'm still a bit unsteady.

The drive back down the nasty road goes slightly faster, albeit every bit as bumpy, as we all brace ourselves and urge Carol, who has taken over the wheel, to get us back as soon as possible to a road that isn't trying to shake us to death.

"Thanks for driving that, Carol," I say as we catch our breath.

"It was selfishness on my part," she says. "The steering wheel is the best thing to hang onto so you don't get thrown around so much."

Back at my trailer, I've just pulled off my shoes and

stretched out on my "couch" to unwind for a few minutes when Ruth taps on the door.

"Ellie, dear, I'm sorry to disturb you, but I've got a problem. Something leaked water all over the floor of my camper while we were gone! I've disconnected the water hose, but I need help taking everything out that's gotten wet and finding a place to dry things out."

"Oh no!" I say, slipping on a pair of shoes. "What can I bring along? I have paper towels, but I'm afraid I don't have a large sponge or anything like that."

"I have sponges and a mop. I just need a hand with hanging up my throw rugs and seeing what we can do with drying up the floor and whatever else got wet. And placating Charli. She's really ticked off at me right now. Her kitty backpack was on the floor. I've already hung it from a tree to dry, but she's not a happy camper."

We arrive at Ruth's site where Charli is perched on the hood of Ruth's truck, washing herself with furious intensity. Ruth hands me sopping wet rugs, a bed sheet, and an extra sleeping bag she keeps around for cold weather to wring out and spread out over the picnic table and benches, camping chairs, her truck, and any bushes or tree limbs I can reach. Thankfully, today is quite warm, her site has good sun exposure, and there's a gentle breeze. Just as I have everything arranged, she brings out articles of clothing that aren't completely soaked, but do have significant wet sections. These should dry out quickly, if only I can find a spot for them.

The hum of a golf cart catches my attention as a man I haven't seen before pulls alongside Ruth's campsite. He scowls at the array of wet items hanging all around us.

"You can't hang your laundry on the trees and bushes," he says in an outraged tone. "Read the campground rules."

"It's not laundry," I say, sure that he'll be sympathetic once he understands what has happened. "My friend had a major water leak in her camper and the whole place was flooded. I'm just—"

"I. Don't. Care," he says, scowling. "You can't hang stuff from the trees and bushes." He accelerates away, not waiting for my response. And it's a good thing, since my next words would not have been kind. I consider walking over to the office to see if Neva Joyce is there. I'm sure she would be understanding and let us keep things hung up, or offer us some helpful alternative. But Ruth is beckoning me to fetch a second bucket and to help wring out a large sponge, so I focus on those tasks first. Maybe before Mr. I Don't Care swings around again to check on us, we'll have things under control enough that I can transfer items from the trees to my own picnic table. Meanwhile, Ruth needs my help right here.

Luckily, the man doesn't return. Within twenty minutes, we've done all we can do to start the drying out process inside Ruth's camper, opening all the windows and turning on the ventilator fans. Charli finally finished her lengthy bath, and is now underfoot whenever we step outside, clearly distressed at the upheaval of her routine. Carol arrives to ferry an armload of damp stuff to the laundry to run through the dryer. Nick discovers that the cold water connector to the kitchen sink faucet has detached and appears to be damaged. Carol squeezes under the sink to take photos of the undamaged hot water connector so we can see what might need to be done.

"That's an odd-looking part," Nick says, zooming in on the picture. "I don't think you'll find that in a regular hardware store. Probably need to go to a place that sells RV components."

"In either case, I think we'll need to head to a bigger town than anything around here," Ruth says. "How far is it to Pueblo? Or Colorado Springs? We should be able to find plenty of specialty stores there."

I search on my phone and confirm that the nearest likely

businesses are in the larger of the two cities, Colorado Springs, which is well over an hour drive away. "Given that you'll be even farther away from sizable towns when you move to your new campground Sunday morning, maybe you need to try to buy the new part tomorrow."

Ruth sighs. "You're probably right. I'm so sorry, kids," she says, turning to Carol and Nick. "Tomorrow was supposed to be our last hike together on this trip."

"We understand," Carol says, pulling her mother into a hug. "This couldn't be helped. You're going to want to be able to turn on your water. If you can get the part tomorrow, we can help you install it before we leave Saturday."

"Of course, you don't have to miss tomorrow's hike, Ellie dear."

"That's okay," I say, smiling apologetically at Carol and Nick. "Actually, I'd like to take a day off from hiking and run errands with you in town. If we have time, maybe we can stop at Trader Joe's. They have some wonderful trail mix that I've been craving." I grin at Ruth and wink.

"And dark chocolate peanut butter cups," she adds. "And soup dumplings. And don't forget the free samples."

I nod knowingly. "Definitely don't forget the free samples."

Carol laughs. "All right, then. Good luck on the plumbing part and the free samples. We'll just have to tough it out on tomorrow's hike without you. I'm disappointed, of course, but we understand." She glances at her husband for confirmation. He nods.

This might be a good thing for them. Both seem far less stressed out than at the start of this week, so having time alone together on what sounds like a lovely hike may be just what they need to get past this rough patch they've been experiencing.

**

When I return to my place, I boot up my laptop to check my email. I'm excited to see a message from Ethan titled "Photo search."

> **Grandma Sorta,**
>
> **I'm forwarding 2 msgs that could be helpful or may only be dead ends. Remember to use the link I sent you to log into the special email account if you decide to respond – don't use your own acct.**
>
> **We're getting more spam/scam msgs every day, so I'll spare you those. Unless you want to get in touch with a Prince from Birazhistan (I don't think that's a real place) who'll pay you $1M to help him launder money. Or want to extend your automobile warranty (make/model unknown). Or feel the temptation to click a link because somebody wrote "Hey there. Have you seen this video of you?" (Pro tip: don't click the link).**
>
> **Good luck & we'll keep watching for stuff that sounds legit.**

I scroll down to the first message he's sent over, sent by Donna Simmons.

> **The woman looks a lot like my roommate from my 1st year in college, Dorothy Causey. How many years ago was the photo taken? We were Freshmen in 1981. If it's a recent photo, maybe that's Dorothy's daughter, because she really reminds me of her.**
>
> **Donna**

I do a quick calculation. Donna & Dorothy must be around 60, considerably older than our mystery woman. Could Lois Lane be Dorothy's daughter? We've guessed the ages of the two people in the photos as being in their 30s, so that's possible. I fire off a quick note to Donna asking her if she has any way to get in touch with her old friend or if she can provide me with more information, such as the college they were attending and where her roommate originally came from. A long shot. A very long shot.

Message number two is from Jay Michaels.

> **Hey –**
>
> **I'm not 100% sure, but he looks like a dude in my bowling league. His name's Ron and I can find out his last name and how to get in touch with him if you think he's the right guy.**

Jay has attached two pictures of people in a bowling alley, with roughly-drawn red circles around a man with a goatee who appears in both shots. In the first, his fist is pumped in the air as he celebrates a strike, the scattered bowling pins at the end of the lane visible in the background. There's a slight resemblance, but I'm not convinced. The next shot is more helpful – the subject and three other guys posing with their arms over each other's shoulders, beaming at the camera. I pull up my best images of Superman and arrange them alongside the bowling team. The beard is quite similar, but the differences between Superman and Mr. Bowler are clear. Superman's nose is straight and narrow; Mr. Bowler's nose is broader and looks like it may have been broken at some point. His mouth is wider, his eyebrows thicker. It's not him.

Maybe something will come from the college roommate connection, but I'm not holding my breath.

Chapter 9

The population has grown considerably since I last visited Colorado Springs back in high school, but the jaw-dropping view of Pikes Peak towering to the west of the city is even more spectacular than I remembered.

"That's incredible!" Ruth has been staring at the snow-topped mountain ever since it came into view as we drove on a mountain highway eastward toward "the Springs" – as locals call the city. "And you say there's a tram railway that climbs to the top?"

"Yes, and you can drive to the top as well. I remember the road was steep with lots of tight curves and I held onto the inside door handle of my dad's car so tightly my hand cramped up. It wasn't paved back then, but I read that it is now. But I'm sure it's still a white-knuckle experience."

She tilts her head to better view the summit. "Maybe we can finish our errands quickly so we can ride the train to the top!"

Oh, goodie. Well, at least she hasn't suggested I drive up there – not yet, anyway. "Look up their website. See if we can still buy tickets for today."

She fiddles with her phone as I follow my car's GPS instructions to an RV Sales and Supplies business we found online. Just as I turn off my engine in their parking lot, Ruth looks up, frowning. "Sold out," she says, sighing in disappointment. "So I guess we'll just go ahead and drive up instead."

I knew that was coming. "Let's see how our time works out," I say, already considering what additional time-consuming errands I might add to our agenda. I've got it! "I'd like to stop at a shopping mall to look for some little gifts for my daughter and granddaughter," I say with a smile.

"Just two more days until you see ... Cagney?"

"Lacey."

"Right. And ... and ... Em!" She smiles triumphantly as I nod.

"Yes, although it sounds like Em may or may not be joining her mother and me. Cagney tells me she has a new love interest who also lives in Boulder and the two of them are off rock climbing or hiking pretty much every weekend. Still," I say, swallowing hard and clearing my throat, "I would hope she would make room in her plans to come down to Denver for at least part of a day." I shrug, looking over at Ruth. "She could bring her boyfriend. I wouldn't mind at all."

In fact, having her sweetie along might make things feel more relaxed. Em was slow to accept me at first, when her mother and I connected less than three years ago. Things have warmed since then, but I doubt she'll ever consider me to be another "grandma" in her life. She has two perfectly good ones already.

Inside the RV place, we strike gold. Although it took three employees to figure out exactly what part we might need, they finally turn us over to a woman whose nametag informs us that she is Ellen Trammell, Assistant Manager. Ellen not only locates the part that perfectly matches what we have in our photo of the underside of Ruth's sink, she also hands us a small plastic bag containing a collection of circular objects, labeled as "Assorted O-Rings."

"You may need some of these. They're only $2.99 and are

good to have in your tool kit." O-Rings. Now there's a name that's easy to recall, unlike "Closet Spud Wrench" which was one of Franklin's favorite old tools he inherited from his father. I could never remember its name without resorting to visualizing a girl in a peasant dress – a *wench* – hiding in a closet filled with sacks of potatoes.

"Ellie," Ruth says, tapping me on the arm, "are you all right?"

I'm roused from my daydreams of wenches and potatoes. "I'm fine. Uh … was there anything else you needed to look for while we're here? Like … wrenches or anything?"

She tilts her head, eyes narrowed in confusion. "Wrenches? Ellen Trummell said this connector should only be hand-tightened."

"Oh, that's right. Well, I'm ready to check out if you are."

When we climb back into the Xterra, I suggest we stop at Trader Joe's next. "I think my blood sugar may be low. They might have samples I can nibble."

"Oh my, Ellie. If you're not feeling up to par, I should probably drive." She hops back out of the car before I can respond. She's got a good point. If I can zone out on Closet Spud Wenches – er, *Wrenches* – then it might not be a good time for me to be behind the wheel. I relinquish my spot and climb back in on the passenger side.

The specialty grocery store not only offers a sparkling watermelon juice sample (I purchase two four-packs) and some mystery dip that Ruth falls in love with, but we load up on a cart-full of other goodies to fill up our pantries. Plus several frozen items to put together a quick but delicious dinner for all of us tonight back at camp. Good thing we brought along Ruth's super-efficient cooler to keep everything chilled!

We swing by a shopping mall where I eventually buy a pair of socks with a brilliant flower design for Em, who has made a point of showing off her colorful footwear at our previous meetings and even during video calls while we were keeping our distance due to the pandemic. Ruth, who can't be outdone when it comes to splashy, bright clothing, helped me select her gift.

For Lacey, I'm delighted when I find a pair of earrings mounted on an attractive card bearing the message, "Here's to the wonderful memories we have yet to make together." Each one consists of two small hoops linked together. Simple, yet elegant.

Ruth has picked up a key finder system. There's a controller, which resembles a small TV remote, and six small, color-coded tags. "You attach a little receiver tag to your keys or eyeglass case or whatever you tend to misplace. Then press the button on the controller with the same color, and the tag makes a sound. You can keep pressing until you locate whatever you're looking for," she explains.

"That seems like something I need, not you," I say. I don't exactly *lose* my keys. I just misplace them. Sometimes I toss them onto my little table and they slide off onto the floor without my noticing. Or they fall down into the bottom of my backpack. Or end up between the car seat and center console of the Xterra. I could go on. Ruth is always quite consistent in stowing her keys in a small basket she keeps on her dining room table.

As often happens in our conversations, she seems to read my thoughts. "It's not that I've started losing things, but Charli has a new game she likes to play. She steals my car keys from the basket and hides them under the covers on my bed, in one of my shoes, or – her latest favorite – inside her kitty backpack, which I think is extremely clever of her, don't you?"

"Do you think she's trying to tell you to drive her to a trail and take her on a hike?"

We both laugh at that. "That's what I figure," she says. "Anyway, I can only think of two or possibly three things I might attach them to, so you can have some of the tags if you like. I just need to make sure I don't lose the controller!"

Finished with our shopping, we climb back into the car and set up the key finder system. I select a red receiver and clip it onto the small carabiner that holds my car's key and fob, which are connected with a single ring. I consider attaching the tag directly to the key ring, but that seems a bit unwieldy. Ruth sets up her keys with the purple receiver and we test both.

"Wow. I'll be able to hear *that* from a good distance!" I say, covering my ears as the receiver shrieks.

One more stop before we start our drive back to camp – the gas station. I'm relieved that Ruth concurred an hour ago that we didn't have time to drive to the top of Pike's Peak. Maybe we can schedule another trip to Colorado next year and we can plan ahead with train tickets on the cog railway. I wonder if they still make fresh donuts in the visitor center on top of the mountain? It's been fifty years since I ate one still warm out of the deep fryer, and I can still remember how delicious it was.

After filling my car's tank, I'm about to get back into the driver's seat when a lady comes scurrying over to me. "Excuse me? I think you dropped this ... key finder." I groan when I see that she's holding out the little red receiver tag I clipped onto my keys not ten minutes ago.

My new definition of irony: Losing my key finder while holding my keys in my hand.

I rearrange my new device so it is attached directly to the keys it is designed to help me find. Turning to Ruth, who is trying not to laugh, I say, "I think I need another one of those tags to attach to my brain."

Chapter 10

We arrive back at the campground before Carol and Nick return from their hike, which gives me some time to start packing up for my move tomorrow. I don't need to leave terribly early for my drive to the Denver area, since I can't check into my new campsite until noon, but the Goldmans want to hit the road before 8 a.m., and I'd like to see them off. My camp set up is simple, so preparing to leave is not a difficult task. I repack my clothing duffel bags, separating out the items I plan to wear in the next few days from the rest, and reorganize my food storage boxes. Hooking up the trailer to my Xterra and folding down the A-frame walls should only take a few minutes tomorrow.

I walk over to Ruth's camper to check on how the drying-out process is going. She's taking advantage of a little down-time to do her yoga routine on a mat laid out in front of her door. Charli is "helping" as usual by ducking under Ruth's body as she moves into various poses. When the cat spots me, she trots over and rubs against my legs, begging for more attention.

"You'll get lots of head scratches tonight, little one," I say, squatting down to pet her. "Everybody's going to be here for dinner. Maybe your mom will even let you eat part of a chicken gyoza."

Ruth twists herself into a new pretzel position. "Even if I say no, I'll bet Carol sneaks a pot sticker to the cat."

Charli trots over to the camper door and meows to be let inside. I open the screen door for her, then take a sniff. "The musty smell is gone. Do you think anything was damaged by the water?"

Ruth starts rolling up her yoga mat. "Not that I've found. Hopefully there won't be any surprises, but I think I dodged the bullet. And if the kids get back soon, maybe Nick can install the new part for my cold water hose and I'll be back in business."

"How about if I give it a shot?" I say. My father was always fixing this and that around the house, so I'm reasonably handy at simple repairs, and this seems like it'll be straightforward now that we have the right part.

"That'd be great, dear. How can I help?"

"Maybe a cushion for my head and I'll have you hand me stuff."

Actually crawling into position under the sink to reach the connector turns out to be the trickiest part of the project. The hose slips into place easily with the new part. "Okay," I say, reluctant to squeeze back out of my spot until I'm sure the job is complete, "go turn on the outside water very gradually, and let's see what happens."

I can hear the water glug and burble as it begins filling the hoses. Then it starts squirting out of the new connection right onto my face. "Turn it off! Turn it off!" I scream, awkwardly scooting my way out of the stream of water.

"It's off," Ruth shouts from outside.

Oops. I forgot about the O-rings. Ruth has returned to my side and quickly fetches me a towel followed by the package of assorting O-rings. It only takes me a few tries to pick out one that is the correct size. I wriggle back into place and reassemble the fitting. This time I scoot far enough out from under the sink to avoid another face washing before having Ruth turn on the water again.

It works! And just in time. Ruth scurries through the door, announcing that it's starting to rain.

I glance at the digital clock above the stove. It seems like Carol and Nick should have been back by now. Ruth received a message from them shortly after noon when they arrived at the highest point above the canyon. They carry a hand-held *SmartLoc* – short for Smart Locater – signaling device with them that can track their exact location and lets them send an email or text message with a link to a map. It's fun to call up a map on her phone or computer to see where they are. They can send a custom text message to her even if they don't have a signal on their smart phones, since their *SmartLoc* uses satellites to communicate rather than cell towers.

"Have you heard from them?" I ask, thinking that Ruth just didn't happen to mention a later message from the Goldmans.

She frowns, looking at the clock. "Not since they reached the end of the trail. They should have been back to their car ages ago. I wonder why they haven't sent a message saying they're delayed. Maybe the rain reached them earlier and they're waiting it out."

Ruth carries a similar communication device, albeit an older model. She's pre-programmed hers with messages like *Everything's okay and here's my location* and *Taking longer than planned, but no problem.* She also has a message for situations where she doesn't need emergency services, but could use assistance, such as a flat tire. Most importantly, these types of units all have 9-1-1 buttons that send a message to the local emergency dispatchers.

"Is there a way to send a text to them?" I ask, knowing that cell service is extremely spotty in the mountains.

She points a finger at me, "Yes! I'll try sending a regular

text message first, in case they have a signal, but yes! I can send a text to a special number that goes straight to their *SmartLoc*." She fetches her phone from the small basket on the table and taps in the message. We sit side-by-side on the couch and stare at her phone, waiting for a reply.

A minute goes by. And another. Ruth changes to the special *SmartLoc* number and sends her message that way. Still nothing.

"Is there any way to know if the message went through?"

She shakes her head. "Not that I know of. Maybe there's something about that on their website."

While Ruth searches for more information on the *SmartLoc* site, I flash back on the situations from my own past when I was in a position of wondering what in the world had happened to someone near and dear to me. It's far too early to assume something serious is delaying them. The days are long this time of year – the sun won't be going down for another hour, and it'll still be light enough to hike without a headlamp for at least an hour after that.

Maybe it's nothing more serious than car trouble. They'll send her a message or show up here at camp any minute now.

"Any luck?" Ruth has set her phone down on the couch between us, sighing in frustration.

"I couldn't find anything." She scowls at the clock again. Twelve minutes have passed since she sent the first messages. The good news is that the rain has already ended – just a fast-moving shower.

"We should drive over to the trailhead and see if their van is still parked there," she says, jumping to her feet and rushing over to the kitchen table to fetch her keys from the basket.

"I don't know, Ruth," I start, but she interrupts me with an angry shout.

"Charli! What did you do with my keys? Bad kitty!" She starts rushing around, searching under pillows and drops to the floor to peer under the table.

"The key finder thingy!" I say, hurrying over to open the kitchen drawer where we decided to store it – a drawer that latches shut so the cat can't get into it. I find the controller and press the purple button. The sound of the alarm is barely audible for an instant, but Charli leaps into the air from her perch on Ruth's bed with a yowl and the volume immediately increases. She was lying on the keys, that sneaky little devil.

"Ruth," I say, wrapping my arm around her shoulder as she pockets the keys and aims for the door, "slow down a minute. Let's talk this through. Take a deep breath."

I feel like we've reversed our usual roles. Isn't she always the one helping me to calm down, to not overreact? "I'm concerned too, but let's think about this." I lead her back to the couch and sit beside her, holding her hand. "Suppose they just have a flat tire or something simple like that. They might have put on the spare and driven somewhere to get the tire patched. Or maybe they got to talking things out and lost track of time. It's still light out. Look – the sun is starting to break through the clouds. Let's sit tight a little longer and see if we hear from them."

Her breathing has returned to normal. "You're right, dear. I don't know why I started to panic. It's not like Carol has never decided to go off exploring and forgot to check in." A tentative smile forms on her lips. "Like the time she was pregnant with Dustin and took three-year-old Gabe to the zoo. He was so enthralled with the monkey exhibit that they stayed well past dinnertime. Nick was frantic when he got home from work to an empty house."

"But they were fine," I say, hoping that really was the case.

"Yes. Nick called me, thinking I'd know what had happened to his wife and child, and I had to talk him down. I don't recall the details, but I'm sure I told him several anecdotes about Carol's exploits from before they got together."

She seems more herself now. "Maybe I'll try texting again, just in case they didn't hear the message notifications earlier."

"Maybe they're in a tire repair shop and it's noisy," I suggest. She nods.

***

Ruth is pacing. I'm trying to suppress memories of being in a similar state a few years back, waiting for word on what had become of a loved one.

"We should probably eat something," I suggest after my stomach issues a particularly rambunctious rumble. "I've got cheese and crackers I can bring over."

"I'm really not hungry," she says, "but you should go ahead and eat."

Maybe I can coax her to take in a little nourishment. I quickly fetch the snacks from my camper and return just as her phone rings.

"Oh no," Ruth says as she picks up the phone. "It says *Emergency Response Center* on caller id!" She stabs her finger at the screen vigorously. "Hello? Hello?"

Unwilling to wait to know what's going on, I move closer so I can hear the caller, placing my ear close to Ruth's. She turns the phone so we can both listen.

"Is this Ruth Erlich?" a woman asks.

"Yes! Are you calling about my daughter?"

"Ruth, my name is Sylvia and I'm with the emergency response center. I'm calling because we have received an SOS message from a *SmartLoc* device registered to Carol Goldman and you're listed as one of her emergency contacts."

"Is Carol okay? What's happened?"

I wrap my arm around Ruth's shoulder and give it a squeeze.

"The information we have at this time is that a man sent the SOS using that device. He reported that he became separated from the woman he was hiking with and that he has been unable to locate her."

"Oh no. That's my daughter. She's *missing*? Is anyone there looking for her? Search and Rescue or..."

"Ruth, I assure you that people are already working to locate your daughter, if that is indeed the person who is missing. We hope to verify that very shortly because it's also possible that her *SmartLoc* was used to call for help for some other party. Either I will call you back or the sheriff's office will as soon as we have that information confirmed. Meanwhile, be assured that the sheriff has already arrived on the scene, and has called in the Search and Rescue teams."

After the call ends, Ruth sits down hard on the sofa. "It's Carol. I know it's her. Nick must have been carrying the *SmartLoc* on his pack."

"We don't know for sure—"

"*I* know. If they used it to help some other hikers, they would have responded to my texts. Nick has probably been frantic, searching for her." She leaps to her feet and grabs her keys again. "I need to be there."

I'm sure she's right – Carol is missing. "Okay, but number one – *I'm* driving. You're too upset. Number two – let's assume we'll be there a while. We need some food and water, maybe a couple of blankets if we're sitting around in the car after dark. Headlamps."

The call comes in as we start gathering the items and are preparing to leave. It's now confirmed – Carol is the missing hiker.

Chapter 11

As I draw close to Thundercloud trailhead, I slow down. Emergency lights are flashing in a throbbing red-blue-red-blue sequence and a person wearing a reflective vest gestures with a flashlight for me to pull off the road just behind two other vehicles. Ruth jumps out of the car before I've come to a complete stop, and runs toward a cluster of people near the emergency vehicle. I take a few calming breaths before emerging and heading her way.

I find that there are only three vehicles actually parked in the small, unpaved lot – a sheriff's car, a sizable pickup truck, and the Goldman's familiar camper van. Ruth is difficult to locate in the bright, ever-changing lighting, but I finally spot her gesturing energetically at a person in uniform standing close to the Pinnacle County Sheriff department vehicle. The officer says something to her, then passes her off to a solidly-built Black woman standing close by. She places a hand on Ruth's back, gently guiding her toward the truck. I cross the lot diagonally to intercept them there. Several people are gathered by the tailgate, pulling equipment from the bed. They've already set up a couple of tables with lights dangling above.

"Fern, I need to go look for her!" Ruth is shouting, pointing toward the trail.

The woman leans over to be able to look my tiny friend straight in the eye. "There's a team up there already and all the other searchers will be starting up just before sunrise." She sweeps a hand around her, indicating the other people in the area. Three more have just walked over and are helping to unload the truck. "They're developing the search plan now, with each team covering a segment. If they don't locate Carol right away, they can call in search dogs to help us narrow things down."

"Ruth," I say, rubbing her back, "they'll find her."

Her eyes flash, her coloring peculiar in the red-blue-red-blue strobe. In a tone I've never heard before, she snaps at me. "You don't know that! Nobody knows what's happened to her." Spinning away from both of us, she turns rapidly, scanning the people around us. "Where's Nick? Is he up there looking for her?"

"Sheriff Gelberman told him to go rest in his van and our Medic gave him something to help him relax. He was exhausted from hiking up and down the trail looking for his wife," Fern says. Her tone is warm and calming.

"But he could have more information on where Carol might be," Ruth counters.

"I'm sure the sheriff will come talk to Nick again if she has more questions for him."

"I need to talk to my son-in-law." Before Fern can stop her, Ruth dashes over to the van and raps at the door. Seconds later, she pounds on it, shouting Nick's name.

I've never seen her like this. Of course she's upset, but Ruth has always seemed to be able to calm herself and focus on a problem. She's been my rock. Now it's my turn to be there for her.

"Excuse me," I say and head over to see if I can help. Just as I reach her, the van door slides open and Nick is standing, hunched slightly in the doorway. The camper shades us from the nerve-wracking emergency lights, but his face is harshly lit by the lanterns the Search and Rescue personnel have placed above their tables. He looks half dead, his eyes swollen and red and glassy, hair poking out in every direction.

"Mom," he says in a hoarse voice as he steps down to the ground and pulls her into a hug. "I looked everywhere. I called to her. I thought she might have come back down to the car, so I hiked down here but she wasn't here. I went back up and kept calling. I can't imagine where she could have gone!" His voice cracks and he closes his eyes tightly, fighting to hold back tears. "If only she had been carrying the location device instead of me, she could have let us know where she is!"

"Why don't we go inside and sit," I suggest.

"I don't need to sit," Ruth says. "I need to know what's going on. If that group that's gone up to search for Carol tonight finds anything, I don't want to be shut up inside where I won't know what's happened."

"How about this," I say, pointing to the seat facing the open van door. "You can sit right there where folks can see you and you can watch everyone." She closes her eyes and takes a deep breath before agreeing. Thank goodness. At least she's *trying* to control her panic.

Nick clears his throat several times before plunging into his story – one I'm sure he's already relayed to the Sheriff and a person he refers to as the "Mission Leader." He explains that they were descending the trail with Carol far in the lead. "As usual," Nick says. "We had already put on our raincoats, since we saw clouds building to the west. When it started to sprinkle, she really took off. She's so much faster than I am anyway, but she always stops to wait for me, so I didn't think anything was wrong at first. But then it seemed like an unusually long time since I had seen her, so I hollered for her to stop so I could catch up. Of course, with the rain, I figured she might keep moving." He rubs his face with both hands. "I didn't hear any answer, so I kept going and called to her again and again."

"Was there a trail junction where she might have taken a wrong turn?" Ruth asks.

He shakes his head. "Not that I saw, but I was hiking with my head down to keep off the rain, so I might not have noticed." He runs his hands up and down his face again before looking directly at Ruth. "We'd been arguing. She was pretty pissed off at me and she said some things ... well, I guess we both said some things that we didn't mean. That we shouldn't have said. So I thought that was another possibility – she was so upset that she decided not to wait for me, even though normally she'd *never* take off like that."

Ruth is shaking her head slowly. "Then what happened?"

"By then I hadn't seen her in quite a while – maybe a half hour or longer. The rain had stopped by then. I figured she had continued down to the van, so I hurried. That's when I slipped and did this." He pulls off the thin wind jacket he's wearing and points to a long scratch down his upper arm and bandages covering his forearm. "Destroyed my rain jacket. I did a number on my knee, too." I glance down and notice the rip on his pant leg for the first time. And a streak of mud that's barely lighter in color than the dark brown fabric.

"Anyway," he continues, "she wasn't here. I didn't know what to do. Wait to see if she shows up or head back up the trail to look for her? I decided to give her five minutes. Maybe she was nearby, but was in the woods, peeing or something. Five minutes. So then this guy shows up. There was still one other pickup in the lot when I got down and that's where he headed. I ran over to him and asked if he had seen anyone when he was hiking out, and he just kind of blew me off. *No, man. I ain't seen nobody for a couple hours.*" Nick frowns. "Then he just jumped in and drove off like a bat outta hell."

Ruth sits up straight and voices exactly what I'm thinking. "You don't suppose he did something to her?" She braces her hands against her thighs and I realize they are trembling.

Nick's face seems to collapse and it takes him a moment to answer. "I don't know, Mom. I just don't know."

"Excuse me, folks." It's Fern again. "Mrs. Erlich? Sheriff Gelberman would like to talk to you now. She'd like to get a bit more background information about your daughter."

Ruth's face is filled with panic. "Have they found her? Is she..."

"No, no! There's no news. I didn't mean to upset you. The sheriff simply wants to hear your insights about Carol. How experienced she is with hiking and how she might react to being lost, things like that."

Nick frowns. "Sheriff Gelberman already asked me those questions. Why does my mother-in-law have to tell her what she already knows? You told us you're supposed to be our advocate. Why don't you tell the sheriff to leave us alone and focus on finding my wife?"

Fern's voice is calm and reassuring. "I understand what you're saying, Mr. Goldman. It can be helpful to get several different perspectives. You've been through a lot today, both physically and emotionally. I would expect the sheriff to want to go through things again with you after you've gotten some sleep, assuming Carol hasn't been located by morning."

Ruth moans quietly. I'm not sure either of them heard her. I take her hand and give it a gentle squeeze. She doesn't acknowledge the gesture, instead getting to her feet and stepping outside. "All right. The sheriff didn't have time for me earlier when I had questions for her, but now she's got questions for me. Fine, if that's how this has to work."

My mouth drops open. I have never, ever heard Ruth speak in a snide manner about anyone. That's more my department if I'm angry. Poor Ruth. I can't imagine how much this has shaken her up. I'm terribly upset, but for her...

I close my eyes and say to myself, *Carol is going to be okay. She's going to be okay.*

Please, let Carol be okay.

Urging Nick to lie down and try to get some rest while we wait for any news, I leave the van and wander through the lot. Ruth and the sheriff are nowhere in sight, so I assume they are sitting in the sheriff's car. Thankfully, they've finally turned off the flashing emergency lights. One cluster of people is gathered around a table poring over maps. I overhear bits of their conversation, with jargon like "last seen point" and "segment four" and "probability of detection." A smaller group stands in a circle, sipping coffee and visiting. They all laugh at something a young man has said.

A trim young woman with a long ponytail fed through her ball cap notices me and approaches. "Are you a family member?" she asks, her voice warm and sympathetic.

"Not exactly. I'm a family friend. Carol's mother and I have been camping and hiking with Carol and Nick all week."

"Nick is the husband?"

Of course she's not going to know everyone's name. "Right. And Carol's mother is Ruth. She's talking to the sheriff right now," I add, gesturing toward her car.

She nods. "Sheriff Kat's great to work with. She's got a lot of empathy, but can be tough as nails when she needs to be."

"Sheriff Kat?"

She shrugs apologetically. "Katrina Gelberman. She's told us to just call her Kat, but Patrick – he's our Mission Leader – has us tack on 'Sheriff' so we don't seem disrespectful. Oh," she says, sticking out her hand in way of introduction, "I'm Hawkeye."

I grin slightly, a respite from the deep funk I've been

feeling. "And I'm Ellie. I assume Hawkeye isn't the name you were born with?"

She chuckles. "Nope. That would be Eliza. The team gave me the name Hawkeye because I'm always finding things nobody else sees on a search or even just when I'm out hiking for fun."

"Does that include finding people?" I ask hopefully.

"Sometimes, yeah. But usually it's stuff, which can be useful in a search, too. Like a pair of binoculars that belonged to the subject. When we located him, he insisted that I keep them as a thank you. I still use them."

"You sound like a good person to have on the team, Hawkeye," I say, hoping she spots something that will lead the searchers to Carol.

She leads me to a table holding large thermoses of coffee and an assortment of energy bars. "There may be some donuts left, too," she says, flipping open a huge box. "Score! I can't believe there's an éclair left. Wanna share it? It's humongous."

Why not? Now that I'm standing here, I realize I'm famished. A handful of crackers with cheese hardly counts as a hearty dinner. Neither does half an éclair, but I'm going for it anyway. And a hot cup of very strong coffee.

We stand where I can watch for Ruth to emerge from the car and Hawkeye shares a few more stories about her talent for finding things. Various articles of clothing, a GPS (which was returned to its owner), part of a sandwich in a zipped plastic bag, and the sole of a boot all turned out to be connected to the lost party. "The search dogs can't be everywhere, so sometimes I catch stuff in places they haven't reached yet."

"Search dogs?" I picture a scene from a movie where dozens of dogs are frantically barking, searching for an escaped inmate.

"I haven't heard yet, but they might bring in one or two teams tomorrow, depending on how the search is going. It'll be super helpful that Carol's camper van is right here, since they'll have plenty of clothes with her scent for the dogs to track on."

We fall silent for a few minutes, slurping our hot coffees and downing the pastry. A thought crosses my mind. "Hawkeye, have you ever found a camera?"

As I tell the story, she's clearly intrigued. "So, nobody's gotten in touch who recognizes the people in the photos? Did your friends post them on any SAR or hiking forums?"

"What is that?"

She explains that there are discussion groups on the internet for pretty much any topic of interest one can imagine. People involved in Search and Rescue – SAR – might have an online forum where people can post questions or share experiences. The same is true for avid hikers, with some discussion groups focusing on trails in a specific area and others talking about gear or safety or a common goal, such as climbing all the Colorado fourteeners – peaks taller than 14,000 feet.

"If they're only putting the pictures up in places that reach a general audience from all over the country or the world, I'm not surprised you haven't reached someone who knows who the people are. Since you know they were hiking here in Colorado, you'll have a better chance if you can reach Coloradoans who hike, right?"

"Makes sense. But how do we do that?"

She pulls her phone out of her back pocket. "Do you have the photos on your phone?"

Hawkeye does some sort of hocus-pocus with both our phones – she probably started using a smartphone in her crib – and smiles when she's managed to transfer the key pictures from mine to hers. "Now, when I can get a signal, I'll post in some places that might get results."

The distraction of talking about our little discovery has been welcome. Hawkeye explains that this stage of a search mission is more *hang around and wait* than anything else, so she seems thankful for something interesting to talk about. I spot Ruth and Sheriff Kat emerging from the car. "Thanks for visiting with me, Hawkeye. And for the dinner," I add, gesturing toward the table. "I need to check on my friend."

"No problem." She heads over to the map table as I start across the parking lot toward Ruth. We're about thirty feet apart when she stops abruptly, then collapses to the ground.

"Ruth!" I rush to kneel beside her still figure and Kat is there an instant later.

"Medic!" she shouts, "Dylan!"

I'm stroking Ruth's short hair, at a complete loss for what else to do. Has she suffered a stroke? A heart attack? No, no! Not my Ruth!

I'm vaguely aware of the sheriff standing up, then gently reaching for my arm. A man crouches down opposite me and places his fingers against a spot on Ruth's neck. "This is Ruth, Kat says to the man. "She just collapsed a moment ago. Eighty-four years old, was very alert and aware when I was interviewing her just now. She's the mother of our subject."

Kat urges me to give the man room to work, and helps me to my feet.

"Steady pulse, breathing is good," Dylan reports as he adjusts her position. Shaking her shoulder, he calls her name and she stirs slightly. "Okay. She's coming around." He glances up at Kat and me. "She probably just fainted. Do you know when she last ate?"

"Her last real meal was at lunchtime," I tell him. "All she'd eat before we drove out here was a cracker and a tiny bit of cheese."

"Hey, Ruth," Dylan says as she stares up at him, a confused look on her face. "I think you fainted. Let's get some nourishment in you, okay?"

Ruth's focus turns my way and I kneel beside her again, taking the hand she offers. "You scared me."

"I don't believe I've ever fainted before," she says, her eyes scanning us. "I thought I was dreaming about a stranger staring into my face. His face kept disappearing and appearing again. He looked just like this guy." She gestures at the medic. "I guess it wasn't really a dream."

Someone has arrived with a handful of energy bars and a small beverage bottle. Dylan helps Ruth sit up and we wait until she feels able to stand with assistance. As Dylan and I help walk her back to the car to sit, she freezes. "I'm not still dreaming, am I? Carol really is missing?"

"I'm afraid so, Ruth. Come on, dear friend. Come sit and eat something. You don't want Carol to show up here and have to take care of *you*, right?"

"Just so she shows up," Ruth says, letting us escort her to the car, then accepting the refreshments.

"You two really should go back to your camp and get some rest," Sheriff Kat says. "Let me be blunt. Looking out for you could take people away from the jobs they need to do for the very best outcome for Carol. I don't expect anything to happen until morning. There's no reason for you to hang around for the next six hours. Go home. We'll call you if anything happens, I promise."

Once Ruth has eaten, I tell her, "I'll be right back." I scurry across the deserted highway in search of a private spot among the trees. The good news is that the coffee I drank with Hawkeye has me alert and ready to drive. The bad news is that I'll never get any sleep before morning. And I'll probably need to pee again about a dozen times before the sun comes up.

Finally ready to roll, I take it slow and easy. My night vision isn't what it once was. About two miles from our campground, I notice headlights about a half mile behind us. Then I realize there's another car behind that one. Maybe some party-goers making their way home at 1:00 in the morning? I turn into the entrance to Skylight RV and am shocked when I look in my rear-view mirror and see the other two vehicles following me in.

"Isn't that Carol's camper?"

"Where?" Ruth asks, the first word she's uttered since telling me not to talk to her while we rode home.

"There!" I point as the van and a passenger car pull past my site to the Goldman's spot. "I think they kicked Nick out, too."

We climb out as Nick steps out of the passenger side of his van, shakes the hand of the man who was driving, and watches him climb into the car. Noticing us, Nick crosses the camp road to come speak to us. The car drives off.

"How are you holding up?" he says, looking first at his mother-in-law and then at me.

"Lousy. And you?" Ruth says.

"Yep. Lousy." They hug, then Nick turns to me and we do the same. "Try to get some rest. I'll come get you if I hear anything." He shuffles back toward his site.

"Would you like me to stay with you tonight?" I ask. We've had occasion to share her large bed when I was having work done on my little camper. When she doesn't answer, I suggest that I set up the extra bed.

"I suppose," she mumbles vaguely.

We remove our shoes before lying down in our respective beds, but remain fully dressed, ready to leave on a moment's notice. While Ruth is in the bathroom, I quietly grab her car keys and the key finder remote and tuck them under my pillow. I can picture her getting a notion to sneak outside and head back over to the trail while I'm dozing. Nope. That's not going to happen.

Even if neither of us can fall asleep, at least we can rest our bodies and our eyes. "Goodnight, Ruth," I say, noticing that Charli has planted herself practically on Ruth's head, staring intently into her face. The cat normally sleeps on a cushioned chair out by where I'm resting. She hasn't let Ruth be more than a step away since we returned. And people say cats are aloof.

Chapter 12

When I open my eyes, I'm shocked to see the glow of outdoor light leaking through the curtains of Ruth's camper. After hearing Ruth trying to suppress her tears last night, I spent hours sitting with her, supplying her with tissues, and trying to find words to comfort her. "I don't want to talk," she said at one point. "Just hold me." So I did. I held her close while she sobbed and rocked silently against me. Thinking back on the five years I've known her, I realize I've never seen her truly cry. I've seen tears pool in her eyes, but nothing like this.

Around 4:00 a.m. we both laid back down. After all that crying, Ruth had to take a decongestant so she could breathe through her nose. I didn't expect to sleep at all, but I must have dozed off.

For a moment I panic as I realize Ruth isn't in the camper. Still dressed, I slip my feet into my shoes and step out the door. Her truck is still here, thank goodness. Oh yeah – I hid her keys. After returning the keys and key finder doohickey to their usual places, it dawns on me that Charli is also missing, as is her harness and leash. Good – they've gone for a walk nearby. That's exactly what I had planned to suggest this morning. Get outside. Try to take our minds off the search for Carol, even if only for a few minutes.

After changing clothes and washing up in my own place, I spot Ruth and Nick walking slowly toward our group of campsites. Charli is wrapped around Ruth's neck, one of her favorite perches.

"Have you eaten?" I ask as they arrive. "I can scramble some eggs and make toast for all of us."

I haven't checked myself out in a mirror yet this morning, but if I look half as haggard as they do, I should probably avoid mirrors and small children. Both deny wanting breakfast, but I declare that I'm making it anyway. "I'm not going to have either of you collapsing again today. You've got to keep up your strength."

The morning is crystal clear and cool, with a smattering of water droplets still clinging to the evergreen needles high above us. As the sun climbs and its light finds them, they sparkle. I bring the food out to the picnic table in my campsite, hoping the sunshine, fresh smell of pine, and steaming plates of eggs will lift the mood. It takes a great deal of cajoling, but they each take a tentative bite of food. Ruth continues to pick at her eggs, but Nick soon shovels his down. Much to my dismay, Ruth offers him the rest of hers and he gobbles those up as well.

"At least eat your toast," I scold. Ruth nibbles at it as I continue to encourage her. Charli is planted in her lap, closely observing Ruth's every move.

Nick pulls out his phone and frowns at it. "It seems like we should have heard something by now. It's almost 8:30 – it's been light out for *hours*. Damn it. Why hasn't anyone called?"

Not five minutes later, as if conjured by Nick's outburst, I spot a Pinnacle County Sheriff vehicle rolling slowly toward us. Someone is coming to update us in person rather than by phone. My stomach clenches as I remember a scene from a World War II movie where a pair of officers show up at the door of a home, bringing news of the death of a soldier.

My face must be reflecting my thoughts, as both Ruth and Nick spin around to see what I'm looking at. Ruth clutches at her chest, while Nick races over to the car.

"It's okay!" Sheriff Kat calls out as she emerges from the car. "I'm not bringing bad news. Sorry to startle you."

"Thank heavens," Ruth whispers. Nick has frozen in place and is swaying slightly. The sheriff says something to him quietly, and gestures for them to return to the table. Once we're all seated, she explains that the search is progressing.

"The dogs have found an unofficial spur trail that Carol may have followed. We've reassigned personnel to focus on that area, but their search has been hampered by downed trees not far from the junction with the main Thundercloud trail."

"What does that mean – hampered? Can't they hike around the blocked spot?" Nick asks.

"Apparently not. That heavy rain we had last week, along with the additional rain showers these past few days weakened that slope. They tell me that two substantial trees have fallen across the trail, and they took out nearly a dozen smaller trees, along with a mass of rocks, mud, and a good-sized boulder. One of the tree trunks is reportedly three feet in diameter, and another isn't much smaller. The terrain above and below the path is steep and currently quite unstable. We've got people ready to try cutting a path through, and expect that to take several hours. Until we've assessed the cliffs and drainage above them to see if additional debris might come down, we don't want folks in that spot any longer than is absolutely necessary, so we're waiting on that. Another team is scouting out other approaches to the area beyond the blockage, since it's possible that Carol moved through there before the trees fell. The needles on the fallen trees are still green and the branches are supple. They haven't been down very long."

A horrible thought strikes me. What if Carol was in the path of the trees when they fell? Being careful how I word my question, I ask, "Can the dogs move through the blockage and tell if Carol hiked farther along that trail?"

Ruth clamps her hand to her mouth and her eyes fill with tears. I shouldn't have asked. Nick is focused on the sheriff and doesn't seem to have picked up on what I'm really asking – yet.

"No, it would be too dangerous to try to send the dogs through that debris. Like I said, we've got folks working on alternative approaches so they can continue to search that area. I'm sure they'll work out something, even if they have to come back at it from quite a distance. We'll just have to be patient. We're also bringing in a drone to see if we can spot Carol from the air, or help find a way in. With all the dense trees in that segment, though, I'm not sure how much we'll be able to learn from an aerial view."

She fields several more questions, filling in details as well as she can for now. "I'd like to speak with each of you individually," she tells us. "Nick, let's go over to your camper and talk first. Ladies, we may be a while, but please stick around the area. I'd like to speak to Ruth next."

Ruth decides that a yoga session might help calm her and goes to her site to set up a mat outside. I carry our dishes inside and focus on cleaning up. When that's finished, seeing no signs of the sheriff or Nick, I boot up my laptop and check my email.

There's a message from an unfamiliar name with the title "photo search."

> **Ellie – i'm friends with Hawkeye & she asked me to post your photos from the camera you found. here's links to 2 threads. looks like you may be onto something!!!**
>
> **Avery**

I'm not sure what she means by "threads" in this context, but I click on the first link and see the photos of Superman looking out at a view and the shot of him with his arm around Lois Lane. "Do you know these people?" the headline reads, and Avery has explained that a camera was found near the Sidestep Trail in the Sangre de Cristo mountains.

The first response below hers asks for details on what type of camera it was, which hardly seems relevant to the original question. Below that, someone provides the name of the National Forest map where the Sidestep Trail can be found. The next response must be the one that Avery was referring to when she said we may be onto something.

> **Almost sure that's a woman we searched for about 3 or 4 years ago. Never located her. Everybody thought the husband did her in, but I don't think they ever arrested him. Can't remember their names right now, but I'll try to look that up.**

Oh, how awful! Here we've been hoping to reunite the pictures with their owner and imagining how happy she'll be, but now this. She went missing and they never found her? Oh, dear. I can't let Ruth hear about this. It would kill her.

Taking a deep breath, I scroll down to the next entry.

> **I remember that. Dude's name was Zakarian. He was on tv several times crying crocodile tears about his wife disappearing. He had some bs alibi claiming he wasn't even on the hike with her when she went missing. Yeah, right. Did they ever find her body? What happened to him – was he ever charged with her murder? Cause he looked guilty as f*****

The next few comments don't provide any additional information, but then I come to this:

> **Anybody know the dates these pictures were taken? Wondering how long before she went missing? Interesting that they found the camera by the Sidestep Trail. Her car was found at the trailhead for Little Brook, so that's where the search took place. Same general region, but not close together. I guess they liked hiking in that area.**
>
> **Her name was Aurora Esposito Zakarian.**
> **Remember her name.**

I skim through the rest of the comments, but after one person posted

> **The husband killed her.**
> **It's <u>always</u> the husband or boyfriend.**

the conversation veered off into arguments about sexism and domestic violence. There's a notification shortly thereafter that the Administrator had turned off further comments on the thread.

Clicking the second link that Hawkeye's friend sent me, I learn that Blake Zakarian claimed that his wife had gone hiking alone the day she went missing. As with the previous conversation, people also agreed that he had likely done something to Aurora and were distressed that he was never charged with anything.

> **The only good thing I can say about this is that the scumbag hasn't gotten a penny from her life insurance since her body hasn't been found.**

The next response claims that he'll be able to collect seven years after her disappearance. What a disturbing thought!

Now that I have a name, I discover numerous articles from several years ago about Aurora Zakarian's disappearance, the unsuccessful search, and even a video of her husband appearing bereft. Whether genuine or not, I can't decide.

When I focus again on the initial news piece about Aurora's disappearance, I freeze. The date she was said to have disappeared – August 19 – was exactly the same date as the final photos in her camera. She wasn't hiking the Little Brook Trail, where her car was parked and where the search took place. She and Superman were both on the Sidestep Trail.

Why was her car parked at the other trailhead? And why did her husband say she was hiking alone that day?

***

My sleuthing on the web is interrupted when Sheriff Kat taps on my camper door. I'm up next. I invite her in and am relieved when she accepts. I feel far more comfortable talking to her here rather than sitting in a cop car.

"What a cool place you have," she says, turning slowing to take in the features of my tiny A-frame camper. "It feels much roomier than I would have expected from the outside. Is that your stove?"

I lift its lid to show her the two propane burners. "The fridge has a small freezer section," I say pointing it out, "and I've got a sink, hot water heater, furnace, air conditioner, and microwave."

"What more could you need?"

"Sometimes I wish for my own bathroom, but that's why we almost always stay at a campground with restrooms and showers."

"Where shall we sit?" she asks. As if there are really any options. We slide into the opposing bench seats by my table. It's time to get down to business.

"I understand you and Ruth are close friends who travel

and camp together full time. How well do you know Carol and Nick? Had you spent much time with them prior to this week?"

I give her a brief summary of the other trips we've shared. A week hiking and sight-seeing in Yosemite Valley, another time we met up in Death Valley. A trip to the Pacific Northwest where we split our time between the coast of Oregon and the Seattle area.

She asks for my impression about how the two of them get along with each other. "They seem fine," I say, hesitant to say something that might give her the wrong impression.

"Specifically on this trip – were they getting along as well as you'd seen in the past? Did you observe any tension between them?"

Either Nick or Ruth must have said something to the sheriff about their falling-out. "Maybe a little. Nothing that struck me as out of the ordinary, though. You know how couples have their ups and downs. Everyone has disagreements now and then."

We talk for a few more minutes as I resist getting into details about what Ruth has shared about Carol and Nick's financial tensions. Carol told Ruth, who told me, so that makes my version third-hand knowledge. No sense in muddying the waters with my long-distance interpretation of what's going on with them.

Our interview finally over, the sheriff leaves to go talk to Ruth again. Sheriff Kat must think I'm pretty scatterbrained. I found it hard to focus on her questions after she brought up the Goldmans's arguments, which she probably already knows were about the life insurance policies. I go back and re-read the online forum discussions, feeling a cold chill run down my spine as I stare at the words.

The only good thing I can say about this is that the scumbag hasn't gotten a penny from her life insurance since her body hasn't been found.

No. It couldn't be. I try to suppress the thought. Nick couldn't have…

It's the husband. It's always the husband.

No! That's impossible. Nick is such a kind, loving person. He couldn't have…

But as for the possible identification of Blake and Aurora Zakarian, I realize the police should be made aware of what I've learned. Aurora has been missing for years – I can't imagine what her family and friends have been going through! Perhaps I can help them find some answers. I watch for the sheriff to finish up with Ruth and catch her before she leaves. Although I get the impression that Sheriff Kat thinks I've become carried away by my imagination and belief in online gossip, she does ask me to forward the links to her, promising to have someone in her office review the information and pass it on to the appropriate authorities, "if warranted."

I suppose if someone had just told me that they've found the key to solving a cold case based on comments posted on the internet, I wouldn't give it much credence, either.

Chapter 13

When my phone chirps with an incoming text message, I nearly knock it off the table as I grab for it. Is it news about Carol?

My heart sinks as I read the note from my daughter.

> **Hi – is everything ok? I thought you'd be here by now.**

Oh my god. Today is Saturday? I can't believe I've totally lost track of ... everything. I was supposed to check out of camp this morning and drive to Lacey's house for lunch, check into my campsite at a state park south of the city by 1:30, then meet her and Em at the Denver Botanic Gardens. How could I have forgotten what day it is?!

> **Lacey – so, so sorry but change of plans. In the middle of an emergency here. Long story. I'll call you in a minute.**

The first words out of her mouth when she picks up my call are, "What kind of emergency? Are you all right?"

I reassure her that I'm fine, although my best friend is in the midst of a full-on crisis.

"That's terrible! I feel so bad for her family. And for her! I can't imagine spending the whole night up in the mountains alone. I hope she's okay and that they find her soon."

Trying to boost my own spirits, I tell my daughter about how experienced and resourceful Carol is. "I'm still hoping she's simply lost. Not hurt. The rescuers may have an idea where to find her, so I'm keeping my fingers crossed for good news soon."

"I hope so."

"I've been so wrapped up in supporting Ruth and so worried about Carol that I hardly know my own name. I'm so sorry that I didn't get in touch with you earlier this morning, and I'm even sorrier that it doesn't look like I'll get to Denver today. I'm hoping things will work out as soon as possible and that maybe I can drive down there tomorrow. But I can't guarantee anything."

She pauses before responding. "I understand. If you come tomorrow, at least we'll have part of a day to visit. But Em won't get to see you. She has to drive back to Boulder tonight."

She sounds even more disappointed than I am. "Oh, dear. I hate to miss seeing Em entirely. Can you take off work on Monday? I'm going to have to juggle around my campsite reservations, but I'll figure that out. That way we can still have an extra full day together. And maybe Em can tweak her schedule? She's working remotely too, isn't she?"

Another pause, this time longer than the first. "We'll just have to wait to see how things evolve. I wanted to talk about … well, we'll see what happens."

"Talk about what, Lacey?"

"Nothing, really. Send me a text if anything changes and we'll take it from there. No use making new plans yet until we know more."

We end the call and I feel terrible. I've been so looking forward to this visit with my daughter and her family, but what should I do? Ruth is in the middle of a terrible plight –

I can't leave her right now! Especially not after all the times she's been there for me. She's my best friend, my sister, sometimes like a mother. I'd love to spend these two days with my biological family, but there will be many more opportunities for that. And, to be honest, my relationship with Lacey is more like that of a relatively new friendship than how I've witnessed the mother-daughter bond of Ruth and Carol. They've shared Carol's entire life together. I only first met my own daughter a few years ago. I never even held her the day she was born.

Now that I'm reminded of the world still existing beyond our troubles, I realize there are other logistics I have to attend to. My camping reservation here ends this morning. I glance at my watch and grimace when I realize check-out time was twenty minutes ago.

I step outside, rehearsing my plea to be allowed to stay here tonight, but knowing that the campground may already be fully reserved. Ruth will be all right for two more nights. She planned to camp here this weekend while I was in Denver, then rendezvous with me at a campground just to the west of Rocky Mountain National Park for the following two weeks. Nick and Carol were also supposed to leave this morning, heading home to San Diego, so they – *he?* – will need a place tonight as well.

I'll offer to switch to a vacant site, of course. Maybe Nick can park his van somewhere along the campground roads. I gasp when I spot a golf cart moving from site to site on the opposite side of our loop – that's Mr. I Don't Care! He's probably making sure all the folks who are supposed to leave today are gone. I spin around and quick-step toward the office, hoping he doesn't reach our sites before I can talk to someone else about our options.

As I bustle through the door, I'm greeted with a cheerful "Good morning!"

I'm in luck. "Neva Joyce, I'm so glad you're here."

She smiles broadly. "I'm glad you're glad! Now, what can I do for you this lovely morning? Do you need a cup of coffee? You seem a bit frazzled."

"No thanks. But I am frazzled." I fill her in on Carol's disappearance. She hadn't noticed the sheriff's car here, being busy working in the office, and was unaware of what was going on.

"I didn't see anything on the local news yesterday afternoon," she says. "It's mostly about what's happening in Denver, anyway."

"Again, I apologize for not thinking about making other arrangements for tonight. Is there any possibility of staying here? I know you have other people arriving, but I don't have a Plan B and I seriously doubt the Goldmans do either."

"No need to apologize. These are hardly normal circumstances." She studies her computer monitor, clicking and shaking her head, then clicking some more. "All right, then," she says at last. "You don't need Plan B because Plan A will work for the next few nights if you still need the site."

"Meaning?"

She smiles. "Meaning nobody has your spot reserved until Monday. I'll extend your reservation for tonight and tomorrow."

"Thanks." The thought that Carol might still be missing Monday is frightening, but this is one less thing to worry about. And if she hasn't been found by then, finding a place to park my camper will be the least of my concerns.

"My pleasure. Now as for site 21, unfortunately I have someone arriving today, so Mr. Goldman will need to move. That's a camper van, right?"

"Right."

"I'm not really supposed to do this, but this is not a normal situation. We should be able to fit the van over by our staff residences. I can move my car over close to the edge of the driveway so he can squeeze in."

"That's so kind of you! I'll let Nick know. Thank you so much for your help. That's one less thing for us to deal with right now." I wish fervently that we won't have any need to make further arrangements beyond these.

The bell over the door chimes and I turn to see Mr. I Don't Care walk through the door. He stomps past me without a word and steps behind the counter. "We've got 19 and 21 still in their sites," he says to Neva Joyce, sounding annoyed and totally ignoring me. I'm guessing he doesn't remember me, or at least doesn't associate me with my own site number since our "wet laundry" encounter happened outside of Ruth's camper.

"I know," Neva Joyce says. "We were just taking care of that."

He grunts an acknowledgment, but still looks irritated. "I've put the new tags up for 21. What're you gonna tell the new folks if that van is still there when they show up?"

"I've found a spot for the van," she says, and before he can question her further, she explains our situation. His expression softens.

"Okay. That's good," he says. Acknowledging me for the first time, he says, "I hope things turn out okay. That your friend is okay." He clears his throat, spins away from us and rushes out the door.

I let out a sigh of relief. I don't know what the pecking order is between Neva Joyce and this man, but it appears that he's not going to veto her offer to let Nick park in an unauthorized spot.

"Poor Henry," she says after he leaves. "Maybe I shouldn't have told him the details. He suffered a terrible loss just two winters ago. His daughter was skiing and went out of bounds, ignoring the warning signs. She was buried in an avalanche."

"Oh, how awful."

"Sometimes he comes on awfully strong to our guests about the rules. He's become quite the stickler for following rules. Actually, he can be downright rude at times, and I've had a few complaints, but I can't bring myself to let him go."

I wonder if his obsession with rules stems from his daughter disobeying ones that might have kept her alive. I feel bad for labeling him *Mr. I Don't Care.* We never know what someone else is dealing with, do we?

"You're a very kind, caring person, Neva Joyce. Thank you for your help."

I walk toward Nick's site on the way back to let him know the new plan, but Henry and his golf cart are already there and the two men are standing outside talking. As I turn to go to my own place, I see Henry step forward and embrace Nick, slapping him on the back the way men do to greet or comfort each other.

Now I need to call the state park campground near Denver and let them know I won't be there for tonight and possibly not tomorrow night either. At this point, I don't even care about getting a refund.

Noticing that the sheriff's vehicle is gone, I head over to Ruth's place to see how she's doing and to let her know that Nick will be relocating the van. Again, she's outside doing her yoga poses. She's always told me that she practices yoga for its physical benefits, but also to reduce stress and help her focus. I wonder, however, if she finds it a distraction or an enhancement when the cat is constantly inserting herself wherever she can be in Ruth's face.

"Are you doing okay?" I ask as I sit at her picnic table to watch her stretch.

Ruth transitions gracefully to a new position. "Not really, but that's to be expected."

With no further input from her, I sit silently, knowing

that her controlled breathing is part of the whole routine. While she's usually willing to speak briefly between poses, I get a strong message that today isn't one of those times. Eventually, she finishes her routine and lies flat on her back on her mat. "Did you get the impression that Sheriff Kat isn't totally convinced that Carol simply got lost?"

Not wanting to make any accusations, I offer a simple response. "Possibly." I wait for her to continue.

"She wanted to know if Carol had seemed depressed," she says, staring up at the sky and petting Charli absentmindedly. She shakes her head. "She asked if Carol had ever tried to harm herself." Her voice is wavering. Turning toward me, her eyes filled with pain and desperation, she asks, "Did I miss seeing something? Did she seem depressed to you?"

I consider the question for only a moment. "No. Not in the least." I get down on my knees beside her as she sits up and we hug tightly. "No, Ruth. I don't believe that for an instant. Carol wouldn't have hurt herself. She was unhappy about the insurance thing, but she didn't seem depressed. Definitely not."

She sobs in my arms and I hold her close, rocking gently. "Come on," I say, trying not to moan as I push myself up onto my feet. I take her hand and help her up, then lead her inside where we can sit more comfortably.

"This waiting is killing me. I'm so worried about my daughter. Carol is everything to me. She and Valerie. I keep thinking: if she's alive, I should be able to *feel* her." She presses her hands to her heart. "To *hear* her in my mind, sending me a message that she is hanging in there." Tears stream from her eyes. "I know that sounds like hocus pocus, but Carol and I are so *connected*. There've been so many times she's called just as I was thinking of reaching out to her, and vice versa." She shakes her head as she dabs at her tears with a tissue. "Carol is my universe. I can't lose her! I can't!"

"Don't give up hope, Ruth. Carol is resourceful and strong, just like her mother. It's been less than 24 hours since she got lost. If you believe that Carol can sense your thoughts, send her positive messages."

I try to imagine the depth of the pain she's feeling, but I realize that even the deepest sorrows I've experienced in my life probably fall short of the prospect of losing the daughter she's so incredibly close to. Even if something were to happen to Lacey, we lack that lifetime of connection that Ruth has with Carol. And I realize the loss of parents or even a spouse don't challenge our deeply held beliefs that a parent isn't supposed to outlive their child.

"Positive messages," she whispers, still breathing raggedly, trying to calm herself. I supply her with a steady stream of tissues and fetch a cool glass of water for her once her tears abate.

"Thank you," she whispers. "I can't believe Sheriff Kat suggested Carol could have harmed herself, or even disappeared intentionally. That's not my daughter."

"I suppose they have to consider all possibilities."

Ruth sighs and dabs at her eyes. "She asked me about the man Nick encountered in the parking area after Carol disappeared, wanting to know what Nick told us about him."

"I just remember he was upset that the guy showed no interest in being helpful and left quickly. Do they think he may have known something?"

"No idea, really. That's all I remember Nick saying about him, too. I doubt there's anything they can do to figure out who he was." She frowns and looks down at her hands as she clasps and unclasps them. "The sheriff also asked about how Carol and Nick were getting along. I think I told her something I shouldn't have."

I have a feeling I know what she's referring to, but I ask,

"Oh? What's that?"

She takes another sip of water. "I told her they had been arguing about money matters. She pressed me for particulars, and I explained about the life insurance policies. She seemed far too interested in the details of that. Now I'm afraid I've given her a reason to question Nick's motive in buying them."

And there it is.

"But I explained to her about his mother dying and the shocking expenses for her burial. I'm sure that's all that was behind his decision, even though he went overboard and should have consulted with Carol before acting."

I need to tread carefully here. "Again, they need to consider all possibilities. You must admit that a half million dollar policy might raise some eyebrows."

She frowns, looking into my face intensely. Since she doesn't say anything, I venture ahead.

"Speaking of life insurance, I've learned quite a bit about our mystery couple."

"About who?"

"You know, the pictures from the camera we found."

"Oh. Right. You know, Ellie, I really can't focus on that right now. All I care about is getting my Carol back safe and sound." The tears start flowing again.

This time she regains control more quickly. We sit quietly for a bit, the cat still insisting on staying as close to Ruth as physically possible. Then Ruth turns to me and says, "You sound like you think the sheriff was right to question the life insurance."

"I ... just think it's something that has to be considered."

"You think that Nick—?" Her expression turns hard, unlike anything I've ever seen on her face before. "I think you need to leave now, Ellie. I can't talk to you right now."

Shocked, I stammer, "I'm sorry, Ruth. I'm just saying it's

not inconceivable that he—"

She gasps. "Leave now!" she says, pointing toward the door.

Tears spilling down my face, I obey her order, offering her one final "I'm really sorry" before closing the door behind me.

Chapter 14

It feels odd to see a gold and white fifth wheel camper set up in what I've come to consider to be the Goldman's place. The new people set up their site quickly, then headed off in their matching gold pickup. When I go to take a shower just after noon, I catch sight of Nick's camper now parked in the driveway of the small house within the grounds of Skylight RV. I see that Nick has backed in so the sliding side door exits onto the lawn rather than toward the tight space between his van and a passenger car. I doubt he could squeeze between the two vehicles.

Turning the shower as hot as I can tolerate, I try to wash away my heartache over having upset Ruth so badly. I only wanted to plant a seed, in case it turns out that Nick had something to do with Carol's disappearance. But now I realize that was idiotic of me. Why poison her relationship with her son-in-law because of a remote possibility that he is guilty of something unthinkable? I'm mortified that I may have damaged my friendship with the person I love so dearly.

I emerge from the stall looking like a boiled lobster and towel dry. What should I do? Go apologize again and hope Ruth will forgive me? Give her a bit more time first?

As I shuffle my way back to my camper, I notice a car pull

into Nick's old spot. A stocky woman with a short Afro steps over to the door of the fifth wheel and knocks. Isn't that Fern, from last night? I stand and watch as she knocks again, then consults a piece of paper in her hand. She looks around and spots me.

Waving, she heads my way. "It's Ellie, right? I apologize that I never got a chance to introduce myself last night. I'm Fern Ellis and I volunteer for the Sheriff's office as a family advocate when needed. First of all, I don't have any major news about the search for your friend, Carol. I came by to see how you all are doing and to fill you in on the current status of the search."

She glances back at the site that Nick and Carol previously occupied. "Do you know if Nick will return soon? I had hoped to talk to all three of you."

I explain the camping reservation situation and offer to go fetch him.

"That would be great, Ellie." What a marvelous speaking voice she has. I wonder if she's a teacher when she's not doing this volunteer work. That voice could calm a room full of first graders who've just O.D.ed on caffeinated, high-sugar soda pop. "Is that Ruth's site?" she asks, pointing toward her camper. When I nod, she suggests we all meet there to talk.

"Um, maybe I should just send Nick over and wait at my place in case ..." I drift off, unsure how to word it.

Fern looks into my eyes. "What's wrong, Ellie? Are you thinking you shouldn't be in on the conversation because you aren't technically 'family'?"

I nod, not trusting myself to explain that Ruth might not want me there.

She places her hand on my arm. "When I spoke with Ruth and with Nick last night, both of them insisted that I let the sheriff and everyone else involved in the search know that you are considered part of their family and not to exclude you from any updates. You are welcome to be part of this conversation."

Biting my lip, I swallow hard. "Ruth may not feel that way today. We had a bit of a falling out this morning." I blink back the tears that threaten to form. "My fault. I overstepped, said something I really should have kept to myself."

She nods and starts rubbing my arm gently. "Ellie, this is an extraordinarily stressful situation for everyone, and tensions are naturally running high. Emotions can be volatile. Ruth told me you are her closest friend. She's going to need you to lean on, even if she is saying otherwise at the moment."

I shake my head. "I don't know about that. I've never seen her like this before." *Deep breaths. Try not to lose it.*

Fern gives my arm a squeeze before letting go. "Give me a few minutes to talk with her before you and Nick come over. Let's see how she's feeling now that a little bit of time has passed. And Ellie?"

"Hmm?"

"Hang in there. Be there for her even if she says she doesn't want your support, because underneath her pain and fear, she needs you more than ever. You just may need to be there for her at a slight distance for a while. And if *you* need support, lean on me. That's what I'm here for."

I can barely whisper. "Thank you."

"Now, give yourself a minute or two and then go ask Nick to come over. When I see you approaching Ruth's site, I'll make sure you know if you should join us or not."

"A secret sign?" I say, trying to lighten my own mood.

She smiles. "Exactly. All right, then. I'll go check on Ruth."

***

As it turns out, Nick wasn't in his van – he was already at Ruth's camper talking with her. As I walk back across the grounds after failing to locate him, I spot Fern, Nick, and Ruth together just outside her unit. Fern spots me first and waves me over. She and Ruth are in the camping chairs with Nick sitting on the picnic table bench closest to them, his back to the table. I start to slip in to sit on the opposite bench, but Nick pats a spot beside him.

"Wouldn't you rather sit closer to everyone?" he asks in a perfectly normal tone of voice. Whew. Ruth must not have said anything to him about what I implied to her earlier.

It's always the husband pops into my brain. I tell my brain to shut up. "Okay," I say, hoping I sound natural. I choose a spot on his bench that isn't too close to him, but also isn't so far apart that I'll draw attention to myself. *It's not* this *husband,* I declare silently, hoping to quell my lingering suspicions.

Ruth shifts her focus between me and Nick, possibly judging the distance I chose. I smile weakly at her while shifting my butt about an inch closer to Nick. She doesn't smile back. I resist the urge to slide farther away again. *Could it be the husband?*

Fern begins, "As I said, there's nothing huge to report on the search right now, but I do have some updates for you. We were able to get a drone up above the area where the trees fell and they've decided it's safe to send in the crew to start cutting a path through. Another team has climbed to the top of a nearby ridge and are working out a descent route to terrain where they may be able to begin searching a segment beyond the blockage. I understand that route involves technical gear for rappelling down a cliff face. Once they get down, they hope to access the region that we've been trying to get to, but from the opposite direction as where the downed trees are, if that makes sense."

Ruth gestures as she describes things in her own terms.

"If the blocked trail is here," she says, pointing to a spot midway along the arm of her chair, "then searchers will be heading this way," twisting around so she can run her hand toward the backrest, "and others will be coming down to join them." She finishes by sliding her other hand down the back of the chair until both her hands meet.

"That's pretty much it," Fern says, "except that they'll be spreading out over a wide area to continue their search, and the two teams will be starting about three miles apart."

Nick grunts. "Have they found any signs of her at all? Are they sure she's even in this area they're about to focus on? Sounds to me like they're grasping at straws." He runs his hand over the stubble on his chin.

Fern nods, her face filled with sympathy. "Remember that the dogs strongly indicated that they were picking up Carol's scent when they led people to the blockage. Their handlers have tried taking them to other possible spots to search, but both dogs brought them back to the same place. As soon as they have even the roughest path cut out that a person and dog can scramble their way through, they'll send them forward to see if the pup can pick up a scent again and give them a good sense of where to look next. I'll let you know as soon as that happens."

"But no other signs?" Ruth asks. "No dropped glove or matching boot prints or anything like that?"

"Nothing like that. Not yet."

All this time, I've been thinking about the various articles I've been reading about that other search three years ago for poor Aurora Zakarian. I can't remember if they used a drone or a helicopter or exactly what, but there was something about scanning the area with equipment that can detect body heat. That technique never yielded anything, but if Aurora was already dead when they were searching, it wouldn't have found her.

"You said the drone doesn't work very well if there's a lot of dense forest," I say, "and I assume that's when it's sending photos or video back to the search party."

"That's right," Fern says.

"Can a drone be outfitted with something like an infrared camera? You know, that detects heat? And could it spot animals or a person? Or maybe a small campfire?"

Fern smiles. "You're right, Ellie. In fact, that's exactly what I going to talk about next. Now, Pinnacle Search and Rescue isn't as highly funded as some of the other organizations around the state, so they don't have their own thermal imaging drone. However, another rescue group is sending over their equipment and an experienced operator. We expect to start that aerial scan this afternoon. So that's another tool to help locate and reach Carol."

"And bring her out," Nick says, leaning forward, elbows on his knees and palms together in front of his mouth, almost like he's praying.

"Yes. And bring her out safely. Even if that means spending another night out, our hope is that the team can reach her with food, water, shelter, and anything else she needs."

"Like medical attention?" Ruth manages, her voice hoarse, her eyes haunted.

"Like medical attention," Fern acknowledges. "She'll be in good hands. Our people are highly trained to care for her in whatever form that takes." She leans over to take Ruth's hand in hers. "They'll take care of her as if she were their own daughter or wife or sister or friend." She looks into Nick's eyes, then mine as she speaks.

Ruth manages a tiny smile. "Thank you, Fern. And thank everyone who is out there looking for my girl."

"Yes. Please tell them how much we appreciate all they're doing," Nick says.

"Absolutely," I add.

Fern rises from her chair and we all follow suit. "I'll check back in with you later today," she says, "but if you have questions or just need to talk, don't hesitate to call me. That's what I'm here for." She sets a business card down on the table.

Before we let her walk away, we queue up for a hug, Ruth leading the way. I'd really love to hug Ruth as well, but I'm not sure if she's ready for that. She's hardly looked my way during this entire conversation.

"Speaking of daughters and sisters," Ruth says as we watch Fern climb into her car, "I need to call Valerie back and fill her in on the latest."

"And I need to reach out to our sons," Nick says, glancing at his phone. "Gabe's sent me three texts and his husband's sent three more in the last hour. Oh, and I see Dustin's left another voice mail." He's tapping the screen and holding the device to his ear as he walks away.

I watch Ruth for clues, dying to wrap my arms around her, but hesitant to upset her further. Her focus is also on her phone. Just as I've gathered up the courage to ask if I might give her a hug, she speaks. "Valerie wants to drop everything and fly out here, but I'm trying to convince her that there's no reason to do that," she says, her head still bent over her device. "She says she wants to be here to support me."

"I can understand that," I say in barely a whisper.

I feel frozen in place, like when I used to play that "statues" game as a kid. I need to remember to breathe.

"I should call her back again," Ruth says after a long period of silence. "I'll tell her how much I appreciate what she's offering, but that both her sister and I can feel her love from a distance."

She stands and finally makes eye contact. "Nick is

absolutely devastated, you know. He could never harm Carol."

"You're right," I say, taking a step toward her. She turns and takes the first step up to the door of her camper. "I should never have implied…"

She pauses for a moment, then continues inside, saying as she closes the door behind her, "No, you shouldn't have."

Why can't I let go of my fear that she's mistaken? That wasn't an apology for *suspecting* Nick, and she knew it. All I was apologizing for was for voicing my concerns. If only I could believe in him like she does.

If I'm wrong about him, can she ever forgive me?

Yet, if I'm right, there's little to no hope for Carol. Please, let me be wrong.

Chapter 15

Fern got word to us last night that the team had broken through the jumble of downed trees and mud, opening a path barely adequate for three people and one of the search dogs to claw their way through. The coonhound confirmed that Carol had continued along the ever-fading path beyond the blockage. But, with fading light and concerns for the dog's stamina after a long shift, no further progress was made in the search.

My body aches after a restless night where I couldn't ever find a comfortable position. I must have looked at my watch a hundred times, wondering if morning would ever arrive. At 5:08 a.m. I give up and pull on the same clothes I've worn for the past two days, then stagger over to the restroom to take another hot shower, hoping it will allow me to feel human again.

The sky has brightened enough by the time I trudge back to my camper that I don't need my headlamp. In the pre-dawn light, I can make out two figures – one diminutive and the other tall – walking slowly side-by-side along the campground drive. I'd recognize that petite woman's walk anywhere. Do I scamper over to join them? I long to, but recognize that Ruth might not welcome me.

I force myself to down a small bowl of cereal, wondering

if Ruth has been eating at all. Under other circumstances, I'd take over a cup of yogurt or some of the chia seed pudding I have chilling in the fridge, but I hesitate to show up uninvited. What a terribly strange way to feel around my dearest friend.

When the sun finally rises high enough to warm my campsite, I settle outside with my e-reader and my phone close at hand. Orienting my chair so I can watch for movement at Ruth's site while also not appearing to be spying on her, I attempt to read, but find that I'm often simply staring at the same page without scanning a single phrase. There's no sign of Ruth or of Nick.

At 8:45, my phone pings with a text message from Fern Ellis, which I see she sent to all three of us.

> Lots of searchers in the target area now. Kat says she'll be stopping at your campground within an hour to update you on her way to the search site. Let me know if you need anything. I'll come by this afternoon.

I assume that means they were able to squeeze more folks past the barrier. And maybe others have rappelled down those cliffs to approach from another direction. I reply, thanking her for the information. A moment later, Nick responds with a similar message. I wait, but see nothing from Ruth. When my phone rings with a display "Colorado Bureau of Investigation," I almost drop it as I fumble to answer.

"Ellie Dwyer?" a man asks. When I confirm who I am, he continues. "This is Agent Edgar Garcia, CBI, Pueblo Regional Office. I understand you found a camera."

I describe the circumstances of spotting the glint of the lost camera and confirm that Ruth and I were hiking the Sidestep Trail in southern Colorado when we found it.

"You're sure it wasn't the Little Brook Trail?"

"Quite sure." I'd never heard of the Little Brook trail until I read about the search for Aurora Zakarian.

"Interesting. I'll want to go over some maps with you to try to pinpoint exactly where you found the camera. Could you bring it in today, along with the memory card?" the agent asks.

"To Pueblo?" That'll take me most of the day to drive there and back. I explain that I'm currently in a campsite hours from that city.

"I understand. Well, let me take a look at a map and see if there's a police or sheriff department closer to you where you could drop them off."

"Could I leave them with Sheriff Gelberman in Pinnacle County?" I offer. "I should be able to do that today. And also, I was using a GPS tracking app on my phone during that hike. I still have our track recorded. I could email that file to you and mark the spot where we found the camera. It may be off a tiny bit, but it's quite close."

"That would certainly work," he says, sounding surprised but pleased. He gives me the email address to use. "I'll be back in touch once I've had time to review everything."

I fret for a moment about having handled the recovered camera without wearing gloves or anything to avoid smearing any previous fingerprints on it, but realize that three years of rain, dirt, snow, sunlight, and possibly a curious animal or two may have also wiped out any sort of evidence the surface of the camera might have once held. The photos are what matter.

Wouldn't it be something if my curious discovery leads to solving a missing person case? The timing is certainly ironic.

***

The sound of car tires on gravel grabs my attention and I spot the Pinnacle County Sheriff's vehicle stopping in front of Ruth's site. Ruth and Nick rise from their seats and meet Sheriff Kat as she emerges. Nick points in my direction, then waves for me to come join them. We settle into a similar seating arrangement as before, with the sheriff settled into the chair that Fern used at yesterday's meeting. I perch ever so slightly closer to Nick than I did then. Everyone's attention is focused on the sheriff.

"The teams are making good progress this morning," she begins. "I told you about the different types of tracking dogs. Our trailing dogs followed Carol's scent beyond the obstruction, but it seems that she may have doubled back and also hiked in several different directions. The hounds are essentially going in circles, trying to follow her track. So this morning we've called in a couple of border collies for air scenting. They'll be able to cover a much broader area far more efficiently than the ground-sniffers."

We all nod. The handlers kept their coonhounds very close by as the dogs followed every step Carol took, noses to the ground. These other dogs, trained to follow a scent in the air, may run a good distance from their handlers before barking to announce a discovery.

"Of course, we also have SAR teams searching this area, some spread out along the spur and others who have rappelled off a cliff to the east. Another team is looking for a navigable path from the official Thundercloud trail up to where the spur trail peters out, thinking she might have tried to find an alternate way to rejoin the main trail."

"What about the heat-sensing drone?" I ask. "Did it find anything?"

She shakes her head. "Nothing reliable. As you can imagine, there are a number of other heat sources besides people up in that forest. Elk, deer, mountain lions, bears, coyotes, marmots, chipmunks. We can eliminate the tiny animals because their heat signature is too small. But you've indicated that Carol has a heat-reflecting emergency blanket with her."

Nick nods, his jaw clenched tight. Another frightening possibility to consider – bears and large cats.

"If she's wrapped up in that when the drone scans the area, it may be holding in her body heat so much that she'll barely show up, so that's a possibility to consider."

Nick is back to running his fingers through his already-snarled hair. "So that was a mistake, carrying those emergency blankets with us?"

"No, not at all. That reflective material will help her stay warm. It sounds like the two of you go out well-prepared. You should feel good about that."

"Yeah. Feel good. Right." His voice sounds dead.

Kat grimaces slightly. "Sorry. Poor choice of words. But Nick," she says, pausing until he looks up at her again, "I believe we're getting close to finding your wife."

She stares at him intently for a few moments before turning her attention to Ruth. "You haven't said much, Ruth." In fact, I don't think Ruth has said a word. "Are you doing okay? Is there anything you'd like to ask me?"

Ruth's head is bowed as she seems to be studying her hands clasped in her lap. She raises her head slowly until she's focused on the sheriff's face. "She would have built a fire. To signal someone. To stay warm. But nobody's seen smoke. The drone didn't spot a fire, did it? Tell me honestly, sheriff—" Her voice, which has been quiet but steady to this point, now cracks. "— do you think my girl is still alive?" Her mouth quivers and a tear slips down her cheek.

I want to rush to her, to take her in my arms, but I'm afraid of how she'll react. I feel like she could shatter.

"Ruth," Sheriff Kat says, reaching over to grasp her hand, "with everything I've learned about Carol, about her strength and courage and love for her family, I believe she is alive. Don't give up hope. I haven't, and all those SAR volunteers haven't either."

She rises from her chair and looks over at Nick and me. I swipe the tears from my face and glance at Nick, whose eyes are closed as he takes long, gulping breaths. "I promise I'll contact you as soon as anything new develops. Take care of each other, all right?"

My eyes are on Ruth as the sheriff departs. She seems mesmerized by her hands again, and looks so incredibly small, hunched over in her chair like that.

"Ruth?" I whisper.

She shakes her head emphatically, springs up from her chair, and marches inside her camper, firmly closing the door behind her.

Nick rises to his feet. "I can't do this," he says, then strides away toward his van.

My throat is so tight I feel like I can hardly swallow. I head back toward my own place, but continue walking on past it. I can't just sit around right now. I need to keep moving, even if that means circling the campground loops for hours. I pat my back pocket to be sure my phone is still there, and try to clear my head.

The screech of burning rubber catches my attention and I stare in astonishment as I watch Nick's van fly onto the road outside our campground. Where in the world is he going?

***

After circling past Ruth's trailer for the fourth time and seeing no sign of her, I'm at a loss for what to do with myself. Surely she's noticed me slowing down as I walk past, hoping she'll beckon me over. As I sometimes do when anxious and bored, I turn to food. Nothing healthy will work. I'm talking junk food. In this case, cookies – treats that I allow myself after a long day of hiking. Four laps around the campground isn't what I'd usually consider a long day of hiking, but any port in a storm, right?

I've finished off a second large chocolate chip cookie and am arguing with myself internally about starting in on a third when a text comes in. It's from my granddaughter, Em!

Sorry to miss seeing you this wkend

I know Mom said she cant see you later this week, but that's crazy. come anyway she needs you

Hope things turn out ok with your friend. so scary!!

Lacey *needs* me? I start to tap in a reply to Em's message, but I'm terribly slow at using my phone's keyboard and sending short notes back and forth doesn't seem adequate for understanding the questions she's raised. I place a call to her instead.

"Hey, Ellie." With two sets of grandparents who've been an integral part of her life, she's never leaned toward calling me *grandma* or anything similar. She already has Nana and Papa, Bibi and Babu. I'm content with having her address me by my name.

"Hello, Em. I'm so disappointed we couldn't get together this weekend, but I hope when things settle down on my end that we can try to reschedule." I gaze at her photo that appears on my phone screen, smiling back at her pretty face. Her lovely deep brown skin and high cheekbones must have come from her dad. But her lips and her smile look like Lacey's. And mine.

"Yeah. No, that's okay. For me, anyway. But I think you need to come visit Mom no matter what she told you. She can get a day off work – I know she can."

Forcing myself on my daughter doesn't feel right, any more than forcing myself on Ruth right now does, even though I'm dying to spend time with each of them. "Your mother sounded quite definite, Em. But as soon as I can think straight, I'll get in touch and we'll find another weekend to get together."

"But she needs you *now*."

There's not a speck of doubt in her voice. "What's going on? What do you mean by that?"

She hesitates before answering. "I promised not to talk about it to anyone, which is crazy. My mom absolutely *hates* asking anyone for help or, like, emotional support?" Her tone rises at the end, making it sound like a question. "But with Nana and Papa gone, you're the only mother she's got left. And this is something where she could really use a mother to talk to, you know?"

I sit down hard. "Wait. Are you saying your grandparents both passed away?" When could that have happened? Lacey hasn't mentioned a word, and we talk several times a month. I must have misunderstood.

"Oh, geez. She didn't tell you? See what I mean? I can't believe she didn't say anything."

Sheila and Forrest, the couple who adopted my baby, are dead. Lacey must be devastated. "What happened? When?"

"So, you know they were like both about 80 years old? And that's like a really high-risk age for Covid?"

"Oh no."

"Yeah. So, they both got sick like right before the vaccines starting coming out. Right before Christmas of '20. So ... yeah."

Her grandparents were slightly younger than Ruth. She and I are so very careful when it comes to being indoors with strangers and we take many other precautions, but you never know, do you? I let out a long breath. "Oh, Em, I'm so sorry. If I had known, of course I would have found a way to come see you and your family." Because, now that my daughter and I have connected, this is *my* family, too.

"Yeah. I should have known that's why you didn't say anything. Mom can be so weird and so stubborn! Anyway," she says, her tone turning from irritation to insistence, "She needs you. Come to Denver. I can drive down for dinner – it's less than an hour from my place to my folks'. Promise me you'll come visit as soon as ... well, you know. With your friend, and all that."

"I'll have to see what happens. If they find Carol and she's okay, of course I can come see you and your mother right away. But if the news turns out bad, well ... my best friend is going to need a lot of support, so I can't make any promises on timing."

"*Mom* needs support," she insists, sounding like she may cry at any moment.

"Em," I say, hoping my tone will calm her, "maybe if you could tell me a little bit about what's troubling your mother..."

A pause. "Okay, so she's already mad at me for snooping. I guess she can stay mad for telling you."

"Well, if that's the case, maybe it would be best for me to wait until she's ready to tell me her secret herself." Now I'm dying to know what it is, but I've got to respect Lacey's wishes.

"She's got cancer," Em blurts out. "There. Now you know."

"Oh, my. Do you know what type of cancer? Is she having chemo treatments?" Oh, my heart. My father died from lung cancer many years ago, but he was a heavy smoker. That was a terrible ordeal for my family. I don't know of any other cancer in my family, but have no idea about my high school boyfriend's family. Of course, cancer can just happen for no apparent reason. I'm well aware of that. As memories threaten to rush in, I order myself to focus on here and now.

I hear her take a shaky breath. "She wouldn't tell me any details, but I know she's been going to an oncologist and cancer treatment center. That's what clued me in – they called to confirm an appointment while I was at my parents' house. Mom had left her phone on the table and was taking a shower when the call came in. I kind of listened to the automated voice message and then looked through the call history for that number."

Kind of?

"Even Dad doesn't know a thing. Mom made me swear on the graves of my grandparents that I wouldn't tell him. She says she'll talk to him about it after he gets back from his conference. Which is crazy. She's obviously known about this since long before he left on this trip. If she didn't tell him before, I'm not so sure she'll tell him when he gets home Thursday."

Cancer. Multiple appointments. If Lacey is trying to deal with all this by herself, refusing the support of her loved ones, that's tragic. And foolish. Her husband is a health professional – a nurse practitioner. I realize that cancer isn't Adam's specialty, but he must be especially well-equipped to help her navigate the medical system. Poor Em!

"Why would she talk to me, if she was keeping it from you and your father?" I ask. It seems like Em is the one who needs and would welcome support. At just 22, she shouldn't have to shoulder these worries alone. Imagine wondering if your mother might die at such a young age! I need to plan to visit as soon as that's feasible. I quickly take a sip of water to try to quell my own panic.

"She said—" Em pauses, clearly choking on the words, " 'There are times in life when we need our mother, and nobody else will do.' "

I pull in a sharp breath. "And she meant *me*?" Her biological mother who gave her up at birth? Who she's only known for a few short years? Em manages *mm-hmm*, which I take as meaning *yes*.

I've never raised a child, but I've seen first-hand the incredible bond that can exist between a mother and a daughter. Sadly, I didn't share that bond with my own mother, who is no longer with us. It was my dad who filled my heart. I see that connection with Ruth and both her daughters, and I envy them. Since Lacey and I finally connected as adults, I admit I've had fantasies about such a bond eventually developing between the two of us. It seems that Lacey has similar feelings.

But what tugs at my heart even more is hearing Em quote her mother while realizing Lacey didn't see that her comment would apply equally to the two of them. *There are times in life when we need our mother, and nobody else will do.* Oh, Em. Of course you need your mother right now and she needs you. I cover the microphone on my phone as I clear my throat a few times, determined to remain in control of my emotions.

"Are you still there, Ellie?" she asks. Her voice sounds stronger than before.

"Yes. Em, I'm going to figure out a way to come visit as soon as I can. If you can't make it to Denver, I'll come see you in Boulder. I know I'll never take the place of your Nana, but I am your grandmother too, and I love you and your mother."

"Thank you," she whispers.

"Call me any time. I'll keep in touch about when I can get there."

I think my head and heart are going to explode. I don't know how I can take on anything more, but I just have to. Lacey needs me. Em needs me. And Ruth, whether she wants to admit it or not, does as well. I've got to hang in there, no matter what it takes. And figure out how to be in two places at once.

Chapter 16

"You got a minute?"

I manage to close my mouth before any bugs fly in. It's Nick. I didn't realize he'd returned. Maybe he drove in like a normal person rather than a drag-race driver.

"Of course. What's going on? Have you heard anything?" My heart is pounding so loudly I'm afraid I won't hear his answer.

He shakes his head. "Nothing. I just need to get something off my chest. Come on over to Mom's place." He turns away from my door and starts heading that way, his head bowed, feet shuffling.

I close things up and head to the spot I've come to think of as our Conference Center. With only three of us attending, I nab the camping chair I always occupied when our lives used to feel normal. Just Ruth and I, gabbing about all the fun we had each day and what we planned for tomorrow. Sharing our thoughts and dreams, our hopes and our fears. Enjoying each other's company and marveling at the natural world around us.

What could Nick have to say to us? Where was he the last few hours? We sit in silence, waiting for Ruth to emerge.

"All right," she says, settling into the chair beside me, "what's this about, Nick? When you took off like that, I was sure you'd heard from Search and Rescue. I tried reaching you, and when your phone went straight to voice mail, I called Fern Ellis. She didn't know anything the sheriff hadn't already told us this morning. And you don't have any news now? What is going on, Nick?"

She's fuming. If you'd asked me two days ago, I'd have told you that Ruth never fumes. Nick looks like he's been scorched.

He runs his hands up his face, through his hair, and back again. I notice his beard stubble is coming in white and I mentally scold myself for thinking about something so trivial at a time like this.

After taking a deep breath, he closes his eyes. "I have a confession to make."

I feel like my heart just stopped. Ruth presses her hands to her chest and looks at me, her eyes wide with shock. "Oh, no," she whispers so quietly I barely hear her. "No."

I didn't want to be right – I *didn't*! What has he done? I scramble out of my chair and kneel beside Ruth, throwing my arms around her. I need to say something – to her? To him? I'm breathless, trying to understand, to figure out what to do. I glance his way, almost expecting to see him blanketed in a dark cloud. His eyes are still closed, but in that instant, he opens them and a look of utter shock fills his face.

"Oh. No, Mom! Ellie! Oh god. That's not what I meant. You thought I … no! No! I didn't … I couldn't …" He starts to sob, reaching out his arms to us.

"You didn't hurt her?" Ruth's voice is raspy and weak and she trembles in my arms.

He shakes his head rapidly. "No, no, never!" He steps forward tentatively, seeking permission to wrap her in his arms. Ruth rises to her feet, reaching back to help me stand as well, and Nick surrounds us both in a tight hug. "I'm so sorry I frightened you. That's not at all what I ... I wasn't thinking. I'm so sorry."

We stand and rock, holding onto one another as if each of us were grasping for a life saver, trying not to drown. Eventually, our grips loosen and we finally sink back into our circle of seats.

"I still do have a confession to make," Nick says, looking quite sheepish. And, in my eyes, guilty of something. Not the *big* something, but ...

"I *think* I'm ready to hear it," Ruth says. "Compared to what I thought you were saying before, anything else has got to be easier to swallow."

"Yeah. Well, it's not good, but it's not as terrible as what you thought before, so here goes." He takes a bracing breath, this time keeping his eyes open. "I was being a total jerk. Carol and I were arguing again about the insurance thing, and I told her to just hike back without me. That I didn't want to be near her." He coughs and clears his voice. "So, it wasn't like I expected her to wait for me to catch up like she usually does. I told her not to. Then I decided to teach her a lesson." His eyes fill with tears. "I wanted her to get back to the car and wait and wait, wondering what had happened to me. To worry that something might have happened and to imagine what it would be like to lose me." He shakes his head, unable to look at us. "So I sat down and just hung out for a while, then took my own sweet time hiking back down to the trailhead. But she wasn't there!"

"Is that when you called 9-1-1 on your *SmartLoc*?" I ask. Ruth is silent, watching him closely.

He shakes his head. "No. I thought she was on to me and was hanging out nearby, giving me a taste of my own medicine. But after that weird guy showed up at his truck, I started to worry. And I realized that Carol doesn't play games like that. She's not a jerk – I am. The rest of what I told you was all true. I did hike back up to look for her, then back down to the van again, hoping we had somehow missed each other. That's when I called for help. Damn!" he shouts, slamming his palm on the picnic table. "I wasted all that time! And I know I upset her. She would never have taken the wrong path if her mind wasn't wrapped up in our argument. It's my fault she's lost."

We sit in silence for a minute. The silence stretches further and Nick stands, looks at Ruth with devastation written across his features, then turns slowly away and starts to leave.

"Nick, wait," Ruth says, and he stops. "Come back. Sit."

He follows her instructions. "Can you ever forgive me? Can I ever forgive myself," he adds more quietly.

"I already have. Do you think you are the only couple who've ever quarreled and tried to mess around with each other's emotions? It happens. It happened with Dave and me, and I'm sure it happened with Ellie and Franklin."

She knows that for a fact.

"It seems that Carol took a wrong turn Friday afternoon. Why? Maybe because of the rain or because she was upset or just because she wasn't paying enough attention. Even if you had called for help hours earlier, I don't think things would be any different right now." She reaches out a hand and Nick steps closer to take it. "Could-a, would-a, should-a. Here we are. We're all struggling with our fears about Carol, and the stress is tearing us apart from each other when we should be joining together for strength and support."

She reaches her other hand to take mine.

"I have two wonderful people here by my side for support. We'll get through this together, my friends."

It's group hug time again. Ruth whispers in my ear, "I'm so sorry I pushed you away."

I whisper back, "I'm so sorry for what I said."

As we separate again, we're startled by a mournful cry

coming from just inside the camper. "Oh, Charli. I didn't forget about you, little one. Come on up here," Ruth says, opening the door and patting her shoulder. The cat leaps up and wraps herself around Ruth's neck.

"Now that I have my complete support team together, it's time to return a few calls. I need to reassure my youngest daughter that we're okay here for the time being."

"And I need to get back in touch with my sons. They're pretty upset that their calls kept going to voicemail while I was out of range."

"Speaking of which," I say, "where were you?"

He sighs. "I drove over to the trailhead, hell bent on joining the search myself. Sheriff Kat almost had to arrest me to get me to settle down and agree to leave. I ended up parking about a half mile down the highway, thinking I might be able to bushwhack my way up to intersect the trail. After just a few minutes of that, it dawned on me that I was more likely to get lost than to help find Carol, so I went back to the van."

"But you were gone for hours."

He looks away. "It took me a while to get control of my emotions."

"I understand."

Nick leaves to go call his sons. Unsure what to do next, Ruth provides me with direction.

"Come on inside, Ellie dear. I need you near when I call Valerie."

I feel like someone has lifted a giant boulder off of me. Now, if only they can find Carol and bring her back safely. Then I'll be able to focus on the other crisis unfolding with *my* family.

Chapter 17

The rest of the day passes so slowly I sometimes believe my watch has stopped functioning. It's reporting that I've taken 6,027 steps today – all while trundling around the campground loops with Ruth – but the hours and minutes aren't progressing the way I think they should. We pause by an A-frame camper that was just set up this afternoon and force ourselves to act normal by chatting with the owners.

"You have the toilet and inside shower option, I see. I just have an outdoor shower that I almost never use," I tell the woman who insisted I take a peek inside. She's obviously put a lot of work into decorating her little place. Custom curtains depicting campers and brightly-colored tents grace the windows. She's pasted a decal on one of the slanting walls that declares, "I'd rather be camping!" The original non-descript floor has been replaced with what looks like hardwood, but is likely a vinyl material. Shelves rise above the sink and two-burner stove, holding functional items such as pots and pans, a toaster and a coffeemaker as well as cute, decorative items. From a curtain rod spanning the width of the camper, she's hung what I would assume are usually shoe organizers. One hanger holds small kitchen utensils, cans and boxes of food, while the other seems to be for socks, undergarments, and rolled-up clothing.

I resolve to avoid showing her the interior of my place. Beige curtains, lighter beige vinyl flooring, my food stored in plastic bins, clothing for the coming few days tucked into a duffel bag, the rest of my clothes stored in my car. Everything I use for cooking and eating lives in a gym bag. No toaster. No coffeemaker. I rely on Ruth's far larger, better-equipped kitchen for luxuries like those.

"Very nice," I tell the lady. Ruth barely glances through the door. Normally, she'd be asking a million questions about the décor as well as quizzing the woman about all the places she's visited, where she's from, what kind of work she does or did. Today – not a peep.

"Where are you camped?" she asks. "I'll stop by to see your A-frame."

I point vaguely toward the far end of the campground. "Over there. Yes, that would be nice. Stop on by when you get a chance."

Ruth takes hold of my arm and steers me toward the path we've been walking. "Take care," I say as we walk away.

"We should get back," Ruth says as she picks up the pace. "Nick might wonder what's happened to us."

I doubt Nick is at all concerned about us. Where else would we be? All three of us, sometimes alone or in pairs, have been walking these loops so many times that I think we've worn a groove in the road. She pulls her phone from a pocket and frowns at it. No new messages.

***

We meet at the Conference Center – a.k.a. Ruth's "front yard" – to eat dinner together. Neva Joyce delivered a casserole to Nick this afternoon, which he's brought over. I shudder at the image of people bringing meals to a family in mourning. He peels back the aluminum foil and we all gaze at the food in silence.

"It looks good, but I'm really not hungry," Nick says. "But I thought you two might enjoy it."

Ruth steps back from the picnic table and settles in her camp chair. "I'm not hungry either."

Unlike them, I'm still in "eating to comfort myself" mode. However, having recently devoured another huge chocolate chip cookie, I no longer have an appetite, although this dish would certainly have been a better choice. "Me, neither."

At Ruth's instruction, Nick covers the pan again and stores it in her refrigerator. He rejoins us outside, sitting in his usual spot on the hard bench.

"Nick, dear, why don't you bring one of your chairs over here? That bench can't be comfortable."

He shakes his head. "I'm fine." His expression clouds over, and I feel like I can read his mind. *If Carol has to sit on rocks or logs or on the hard, damp ground, why should I sit in a comfy chair?*

Or maybe that's just my own conscience.

We sit silently for the most part, any attempts at starting up a conversation falling flat almost immediately. I fret about my daughter and granddaughter, trying to weigh Ruth's need for me here against their needs. Earlier this afternoon, I explored options for driving to Denver and finding a place to stay. The State Park campground I was supposed to stay at last night and tonight is fully booked through the end of September. I couldn't find any other camping possibilities, but there's always a hotel. Perhaps I could book two nights, parking my trailer in a hotel lot, then meet back up with Ruth wherever she ends up next. Would she move on to our reserved sites at the lakes near Rocky Mountain National Park if things are resolved here before our time there is up?

Listen to me. "If things are resolved" – what a cold way of thinking about learning if Carol is alive or dead. I feel ashamed of myself.

"Look at that sky," Ruth says, drawing me out of my thoughts.

The light is fading and the scattered clouds above us are turning pink. "I don't think it's going to rain tonight," Nick says. "Thankfully."

We nod in agreement. It rained Friday afternoon while he and Carol were hiking, and there was another brief shower yesterday, much to our dismay. It looks like we've lucked out today. The downside is that the clouds have continued dissipating and the forecast calls for clear skies overnight. Clear skies around here often translate into colder nighttime temperatures. I can feel the warmth of the day fading. I offer to bring a sweater out for Ruth, which she accepts gratefully. "I'm going to fetch another layer from my place," I say. "How are you doing, Nick?" He's shoved his hands between his knees, obviously feeling chilled.

"I'm fine."

Back at my camper, I pull a fleece jacket over my head and am walking toward Ruth's place when my phone chimes. I hear a chorus of chirps and dings from their phones as I yank mine out of my pocket.

Carol has been found and is ok. No injuries. Fern is on her way to fill you in on details.

I dash to join Ruth and Nick as they yelp with joy. "She's okay!" Ruth yells, throwing her arms around Nick, who is on his feet, his hands covering his face, trembling. I join them, repeating, "She's okay! She's okay!"

Nick's phone, which is lying on the ground, chirps again. He seems so overwhelmed that I don't think he's heard it, so I pick it up and hand it over. His face is wet with tears, which he swipes away so he can see the screen. With a snort, he reads the new message.

"It's from Sheriff Kat again," he says, shaking his head but grinning broadly. "She says, 'Don't show up here until I contact you tomorrow morning! They won't hike down until then. Catch up on your sleep tonight. You'll see your wife soon.' "

Now we're all crying, but our laughter soars to the sky.

Chapter 18

When Fern Ellis arrived last night, she let us know more details about what would be happening next. Two members of the Search and Rescue team would spend the night with Carol. She was tired, hungry, and dehydrated when SAR found her, but Fern assured us that they had provided her with warm drinks, a hot meal, a cozy sleeping bag and tent, along with plenty of hugs and compassion for what she'd been through.

We're disappointed that Carol will have to spend a third night out there, but are relieved that she is no longer alone.

"She's in good spirits," Fern said. "With a good night's rest, they report that Carol appears to be capable of hiking out under her own power. They'll have a hot breakfast in the morning, then take their time coming down with her. They'll radio us when they set out, so I'll be able to relay that to you. They said to expect the hike out to take two to three hours, depending on how Carol's energy is holding up, so I'd anticipate something like 10 a.m. at the very earliest."

With the drive to the trailhead being less than 40 minutes, we can be there in plenty of time to meet Carol and her rescuers when they arrive at the parking area. Nick and Ruth wanted to head over there at the crack of dawn, then dash up the trail to meet them. I made them promise to obey

Sheriff Kat's orders not to show up until mid-morning. There's still a strong possibility they won't want to stay put at the trailhead. She may have to handcuff them to a tree.

Just kidding. Sort of.

We're all slurping our third cups of coffee as we hover around Ruth's camper when Neva Joyce and Henry (Mr. I Do Care After All) roll up in the golf cart just after 7:00 a.m. "We brought you a few things to celebrate," Neva Joyce announces as they unload items from the back – assorted bags of chips, tubs of guacamole and onion dip, and a covered cake pan. And a six-pack of beer.

"How did you know?" I ask, quickly realizing that Nick must have reported the good news when he returned to his camper parked in her driveway. Yet, that was around 10:00 last night. When did they put all this together?

"I hope Carol likes chocolate," Neva Joyce says, handing over the cake.

"It's her favorite," Ruth and Nick reply in unison.

"This is home-made," Ruth says. "When did you have time to bake this?"

Neva Joyce shrugs. "I baked it last night and frosted it this morning. Henry's putting together a big pan of his famous chicken enchiladas."

Henry nods. "Just call the office about a half hour before you plan to eat and I'll have them all heated up and ready to go."

Nick looks like he may cry again. "This is so incredibly kind of both of you. I really didn't intend for you to go to all this trouble when I talked to you last night, Neva Joyce. And Henry – that will be amazing. I know Carol will love it."

"We all will," I chip in. Ruth has hardly eaten since Friday evening, I doubt Nick has, and I've been stress-eating sugary junk. Except for this morning, since I'm too excited to down anything but coffee so far.

They stay and chat for a little while – a welcome

distraction. We try to focus on generic topics like sports, the weather, and travel. At 7:42, we race to snatch up our phones which just sounded almost simultaneously. The rescue party is starting down!

"We've got to go!" Nick announces.

"We'll help put the food inside and get out of your hair," Neva Joyce says, gathering up her cake while the rest of us – excluding Nick – pick up the rest and set everything on Ruth's kitchen counter or in her refrigerator. Nick is too fidgety to do anything but pace, edging toward my car.

"Okay. Remember to call or text so I can have the enchiladas hot for you when you're ready."

Nick is backing toward my Xterra, gesturing for us to follow him.

"Nick," I say as I pull my keys from my pocket, "they won't be down to the trailhead until at least 9:45. We have plenty of time."

"I know, I know," he says, walking swiftly the last twenty feet and climbing into the back seat. Ruth is only a few steps behind him and quickly scrambles into the front.

It's a good thing I'm the designated driver. If either of them was in control, we'd be setting land speed records on our way to meet Carol.

***

The scene at the trailhead is considerably different than when I was here Friday night. Fewer vehicles, only a handful of people hanging around, and of course it is daylight. Sheriff Kat greets us as we emerge from my car, emphasizing that we are all to remain down here in the parking area rather than heading up the trail. "Don't complicate things," she says. "People have been putting in long shifts and they're tired. I don't want even the slightest possibility of having one of you twist an ankle or any other problem for them to deal with. Are we good?"

The serious look on her face allows for no arguments. "We're good," Nick says, with Ruth and me echoing. An old maxim crosses my mind: *It ain't over till it's over.* Yogi Berra, I believe. While I'm enormously optimistic about today's outcome, there's no reason to risk complicating things.

We hang around and wait. And drink coffee. And turn down offers of energy bars and mandarin oranges and cold pizza with all the toppings picked off.

Suddenly, a radio crackles. I can't make out what's being said as Sheriff Kat holds her walkie-talkie to her ear, but she's smiling as she replies. Everyone stops what they're doing and turns toward the trailhead.

"Carol!" Nick shouts, rushing forward to take his wife in his arms. They grab ahold of each other like they'll never let go. Ruth is displaying incredible control, holding back. I glance her way and realize she's holding her hands over her face, sobbing silently, her features almost seeming to melt.

"Ruth," I say, my hand rubbing her upper back gently, "she's okay. Your daughter is okay."

Carol looks a bit bedraggled, with mud smeared on her seat and hair snarled, but otherwise fine.

Just then Carol looks our way, gives her husband's arm a squeeze, then scurries over to her mother. They fall into each other's arms, rocking and cry-laughing. I feel a tear meander down my cheek. Nick comes close, but gives them a moment before wrapping his arms around both of them.

"Ellie, get in here," Ruth says, reaching one arm out to pull me into their cocoon. I close my eyes and take in all the love and joy of our embrace. This is one happy ending. Soon I'll need to engulf myself in a different mother-daughter story, but for this moment, I'll focus on the wonderful news in the lives of these people who mean so much to me. Ruth, who I love as a dear friend; Carol, who feels like a sister to me.

And Nick. I offer up a silent apology for questioning his genuine love for his wife. Ruth will never say a word to them about our falling out, and I owe her thanks for her forgiveness.

Eventually our cluster opens up and we make the rounds, thanking everyone still present for all they've done to bring us to this wonderful moment. I'm especially pleased to see that Hawkeye was one of the rescuers who spent the night with Carol and hiked out with her.

"You realize what a difference you've made in our lives, don't you?" I say to her. "Thank you. And thanks also for having your friend post those photos for me. Did you hear what happened?"

She had not. Between working shifts in Carol's search and taking care of her "regular life" in between, she hadn't paid any attention to emails or other messages that didn't seem crucial. I tell her about Superman – Blake Zakarian – and his wife who went missing. About the mystery of her car being found at one trailhead, where Blake said she was hiking alone, yet her camera and photos of her husband indicated that they had been hiking in an entirely different location on the day she disappeared.

"That's amazing," Hawkeye says. "It sounds to me like Superman must have done something to her. Did they ever find any signs of her?"

I shake my head. "No, but I assume they only searched the area where they thought she had been. I've been looking at detailed maps, and the two trails were a good thirty miles apart with no connecting trails between them. I can't imagine the search was ever extended that far away."

"No, it wouldn't be with no reason to suspect she had been over there. Was the husband ever arrested?" She leans closer and lowers her voice. "They always consider the husband or boyfriend as a possible suspect."

It's always the husband. I glance over at Nick. *Nope. Not always.*

"From what I've read about the case, they took him in for questioning but had to release him. He had an alibi, saying he was with his brother the whole day."

"Which was obviously a lie, since you found photos of Superman at the overlook on *your* trail. So," she says as she reaches for her pack on the ground, "what happens next?"

I shrug. "I haven't heard anything back from the authorities. I hope the pictures are enough for them to open the case back up and figure out what happened to Aurora. I'm sure her parents and friends would like to know. And if Superman did something to her, arrest him."

Someone taps out a couple of beeps on a car horn. "Oops, that's my ride," Hawkeye says, shouldering her pack. "Gotta go."

We hug briefly and I wish her well. "Thanks again. Go home and get some rest," I call to her as she jogs over to her friend's car.

"No rest for the wicked!" she calls back as she climbs in and they drive away, the large communications van following them out onto the highway.

Looking around the lot, I see that we're down to just the sheriff's car and mine. I join my friends who are chatting with Sheriff Kat.

"No, there's no charge for their services," Kat is saying as I walk up. "So, certainly, any donation you'd like to give would be very much appreciated but is definitely not required. Thank you for asking." She hands Carol a business card, saying, "Here's the contact information for Pinnacle Search and Rescue. I couldn't ask for a more dedicated group of volunteers."

"I'm so grateful to them. And to you," Carol says.

Nick adds, "And Fern. She was always so calm and

patient with us, even when I was having a meltdown. I'd hoped she'd be here to thank in person, but can you let her know how much we appreciated her help?"

"We do have her number," Ruth reminds him. "We can call her when we get back to camp."

I glance at Carol as she sways slightly, and reach out for her arm to steady her. "I think we should get you home. Are you hungry? There's a feast waiting for us back at the RV camp."

"They fed me a great breakfast," she answers, "but yeah, I could eat again. And I'd really like to sit down on something with a cushion!"

Nick wraps his arm around her shoulder. "Let's get you in the car."

Ruth and I say a final goodbye to Sheriff Kat and we all climb into my Xterra. As I drive, I glance back at the Goldmans in my rear-view mirror now and then. Nick has scooted over to the middle so he can hold Carol in his arms. They whisper quietly the entire way back, while Ruth looks over her shoulder frequently, smiling broadly at the sight of them.

Chapter 19

First priority when we have cell phone service again is to set up a conference call with Carol's sister and two sons, who all insisted they needed to actually hear her voice when we let them know last night that she had been found. We huddle around the table in Ruth's camper, Nick's phone set in the middle. The cat moves from lap to lap and sniffs at the phone as she makes her rounds.

We held off on asking Carol many questions about her ordeal until we could hold this family group discussion, focusing mostly on how she's feeling and what she needs. Back at the trailhead, she told us that she was more worried about how all of us were doing than about herself. "I kept trying to send all of you a telepathic message that I was okay and not to worry. I wanted so much to get back to you. I'm sorry I put you through all that."

Naturally, that resulted in more long hugs and Nick murmuring in her ear, "You have nothing to apologize for. *I'm* sorry. This was my fault." And she would reply, "No, *I'm* sorry!" Ruth, who had been laughing and crying in equal measures since her daughter had arrived, piped in, "No, *I'm* sorry!" which elicited giggles and more declarations of "No, *I'm* sorry!" Carol switched it up by declaring, "I'm Spartacus!" echoed by each of us. This crazy family – even after what we've been through these last few days, humor and playfulness remain part of their essence.

After reassurances from Carol that she is feeling fine, Gabe prompts her for details of her experience. "Mom, how did you end up where you did? If the rescuers couldn't get past those downed trees, how did you?"

She nods at the phone. "My first mistake was that I wasn't paying attention to where I was. It was raining and I never considered there was more than the one trail. Obviously, I turned onto the spur and just kept going for maybe five minutes or so before I looked around and realized the terrain was wrong. I had my phone drawing a track of our hike, so as soon as I looked at that, I saw that I needed to backtrack to be on the right trail. Right about then the rain started coming down harder, so I tucked myself under the branches of a cluster of trees, figuring it might pass through quickly. Which it did."

Carol has her arms resting on the table as she speaks, and I notice they're crisscrossed with dozens of scratches. Nothing deep – I've done far worse to my arms when gardening.

"But while I was waiting, I heard rumbling," she continues.

"Thunder?" Ruth asks.

Carol shakes her head. "It didn't sound quite right. So, the rain was letting up and I headed back the way I had come, but then I thought I'd taken another wrong turn, because the narrow trail I was following came to a dead end at a huge pile-up of fallen trees and rocks. When I checked my phone's map, I realized this mess had just happened. I had walked right through that spot ten or fifteen minutes earlier!"

Ruth has a hand over her mouth, her eyes wide. Nick, who has been sitting so close to his wife that they've practically melded together, leans over and kisses her on the head. If she hadn't paused to wait for the rain to subside, she might have been in the path of the immense trees when they toppled!

"I could see there was no way to climb over the debris," Carol says, "so I looked for a way around. Trust me, that wasn't going to happen. The hillside was too steep, both above and below the path, and the forest too dense, with lots of deadfall from over the years. Besides, I was worried that more trees and rocks might have loosened above me with the rain."

She describes how she reversed course again, hoping the spur trail might eventually reconnect with the Thundercloud Trail. When it petered out at a viewpoint over a gorge, she began searching for her own way to cut back through the forest to intersect the path she and Nick had followed that morning.

"I could see from my phone's map that some areas would just cliff out – those weren't an option. There were other routes that didn't look terribly steep, but turned out to be covered with crumbly rocks and outcroppings and more deadfall. I finally realized that I was likely to get hurt and impossible to locate if I kept trying to bash my way through all the obstacles. So I made my way back up to the spur trail and settled down in a place where I had a little shelter from the wind or rain and a nice log to sit on."

She grins and gestures downward. "You could probably identify my log by the imprint it left in my butt."

Her son, Dustin, who has been almost silent up until now, moans. "T.M.I., Mom."

I whisper in Ruth's ear, "Too Much Information."

She whispers back, "I knew what it meant."

Carol rushes through the rest of her story, explaining that there wasn't much to it. She lost track of time and even of what day it was. Her attempts to start a fire were frustrating, as the recent rains had left everything damp. "I'd manage to light a few tiny twigs, but it would go out before I could get a twig even the size of my little finger to catch."

We tell her about the drone search, with its heat-seeking scanner and all agree that it may have missed recognizing her as a "large animal" because she often had her reflective emergency blanket wrapped around her. "I think I heard it!" she says. "One morning – or it could have been afternoon; I can't remember – I thought I was hearing a lot of buzzing bees. I looked around for a flowering bush or anything that might attract bees, but then it seemed like they'd flown away. That must have been a drone. I guess I should have been waving my blanket instead of wearing it."

"Weren't you scared?" Valerie asks.

Her sister replies instantly. "Not so much scared as frustrated and worried about all of you guys and what I was putting you through. Although, when I still hadn't heard anyone coming to help me by the second night, I started worrying about being nearly out of water and food, and dreading the long hours of darkness. So, yeah, I guess I felt scared by then. I was afraid of becoming hypothermic if I didn't stay awake and move around all night. I talked to myself and sang, and hummed until my voice gave out."

Nick pulls her closer.

"But I made it through another night!" she declares. "And by that afternoon, I thought I heard voices, so I started blowing my whistle, but I didn't hear anything else for hours. I tried yelling, but my throat was so parched I could barely make a sound." She sits up straighter, her face flushed with excitement. "But then a dog came dashing through the woods over to me and was barking and people were shouting and it was so wonderful after not seeing another soul for more than 48 hours!"

Valerie asks her sister many more questions, which Carol patiently answers. I say *patiently*, because Valerie isn't as much of an outdoors person, and isn't familiar with things like how Nick and Carol's *SmartLoc* works to send and receive messages or how a phone can draw a line on a map depicting where Carol had been hiking.

"Maybe we should wrap this up for now," Ruth suggests. "I think Carol is fading."

We all say our goodbyes and Carol promises to call each of her remote family members within the next several days.

"Do you need to take a nap, honey?" Nick asks. "We can re-heat the enchiladas for later."

"Eat now, nap later!" she answers. "I'm famished – again!"

We decide to enjoy the warmth of the sun by eating outside at the picnic table. Ruth supplies folded-up towels for padding to sit on. "Thanks, Mom. My butt has had enough of sitting on hard surfaces for a while!"

We chow down. Henry's enchiladas are fantastic and he's supplied us enough to feed a dozen people. The chocolate cake is decadently rich, but despite each of us taking a large piece, there's plenty left. Ruth brings out some plastic containers so we can split up the leftovers. She manages to spoon out nearly all of the delicious sauce from the enchilada pan. Carol offers to wash it, along with the cake dish.

"Don't be silly, sweetie. One of us will take care of them. You and Nick should just go relax. I know you want some time together, just the two of you."

They haven't stopped holding hands, sitting so close they seem joined at the hip, gazing into each other's eyes, and hugging since Carol arrived at the trailhead this morning. Yes, I think they want some alone time.

"But first, a shower," Carol says. She gives Nick's arm an affectionate squeeze. "I stink."

"You can use mine," her mother offers, pointing toward her camper, but Carol shakes her head.

"I'll use the campground shower. I plan to soak under that lovely hot water for a long, long time."

They accept their packages of food and head off toward the showers and their van, pressed close together, arm in arm, stepping in perfect unison. "They'd do great in a three-legged race," I comment. "Too bad the showers are in separate men's and women's restrooms."

"I'm not entirely sure that'll stop them from sharing a stall."

Oh my.

Ruth and I carry the remaining food inside – bags of chips and bowls of dip. I step back out to retrieve the dirty pans only to discover that Charli has stuffed herself into the enchilada pan, and is diligently licking the remaining sauce from its edges.

"Oh, Charli. I don't think you're supposed to be up there."

Ruth emerges to see what the cat is up to. "Oh, well. Normally I'd scold her and make her get down, but she's doing a fine job of pre-washing. And she's been such a comfort to me these past few days."

The cat looks up at us, stands, turns in a slow circle, carefully arranges herself back inside the pan, and continues "cleaning" it.

"Cats and boxes," Ruth says, chuckling.

"If it fits, she sits." I place my arm around my dear friend and smile as she returns the gesture. It feels so wonderful to be enjoying each other's company again. Unfortunately, it's already past check out time and someone is going to be moving into my campsite this afternoon. With all the excitement, I almost forgot. Now I need to load up and head out. If only I knew where I'm going to camp tonight!

I should head to Denver. Find a hotel in the general area of my daughter's home, park my trailer, and firm up a plan to go see her.

Although I'm reluctant to spoil Ruth's joyous mood, I

need to tell her that I don't know exactly when I'll be joining her at the campground near Rocky Mountain National Park for the next segment of our Colorado trip.

"Ruth, I've got news about my daughter."

Chapter 20

Before departing, I'm able to pull my car and trailer mostly off the side of the campground road by Ruth's site. "I really wanted to tell Carol and Nick goodbye," I say as Ruth and I hug.

"I'll give them your love," she says, stepping back and smiling. "They didn't respond to my text message, and I'm certainly not going to go knock on their door." She wiggles her eyebrows suggestively and we both giggle like schoolgirls. I'm sure I'm blushing, but she simply looks delighted.

Before rolling out onto the highway, I check my phone for a reply to my earlier message to Em asking her advice on how to let her mother know I intend to show up for our visit, albeit a couple of days late.

> **great! call her on her cell. tell her to pick a restaurant for tonight & to take tomorrow off**

That's a lovely plan, but I have no idea how Lacey will react to it. I send a thumbs-up symbol to Em, wondering if I should call now, or wait until I'm closer to metro-Denver where I'll have phone service again. Knowing that I'll be fretting until I make a move, I tap my daughter's phone number. *Don't overthink this.*

"Hi, Ellie! Any update on your missing friend?"

Briefly, I fill Lacey in on the wonderful news, then take the plunge. "That's not the only reason I'm calling. I'd feel terribly disappointed if I couldn't see you and Em on this trip. Actually, I'm heading your way right now and will be in Denver by early this afternoon. I know this is extremely short notice, but can we meet somewhere for dinner? Em already texted me that she can drive down from Boulder, and I understand Adam is at a conference in Florida. So..."

"Uh, it sounds like you and Em have been talking already." She doesn't sound angry – just wary. "Have you two been plotting behind my back?"

I decide to keep it light for now and not reveal that I know her secret. Chuckling, I say, "Of course we have. Isn't that what grandmothers are supposed to do? Make our grandchildren's wishes come true? Or am I confusing that with fairy godmothers?"

She lets out a long breath. "That sounds like something Mom would say." She's attempting to match my upbeat tone, but I hear the sadness in her voice.

"So, is it a date?" I ask, sticking to my role of ignorance about anything Em has disclosed, including the loss of her adoptive parents.

After a beat, she agrees. "Would it work for you if we order takeout and eat at my house?"

"That would be perfect!" I had planned to use our dinner meeting to get her to agree to more private time tomorrow, but that felt like a gamble. This might provide an opening to talk about her medical condition even if she avoids an additional get-together with me.

"Great. Would 6:30 be too early? Where will you be staying?"

I glance up and see Henry heading toward me in the golf cart. Uh oh. I'm really not parked in an acceptable spot. I roll down my window and point to my phone, then hold a finger up. *Just one minute.*

He nods and waves as he rolls on past.

"Sorry. I thought I might need to move my car," I tell her. "Actually, I haven't made a reservation yet. I figured there'll be lots of choices for hotels once I get into town."

"Oh. I thought you had your camper with you. Aren't you staying at Chatfield State Park?"

"Well, that was for this past weekend. And you know what happened with that plan. Fortunately, my camper is pretty tiny, so I'm sure I'll be able to leave it folded down in a hotel parking lot while I'm visiting."

"Don't be silly, Ellie. Stay at my house tonight. You can park on the street – that's not a problem. We have a guest room with its own bath. Oh," her voice perks up, "maybe Em can spend the night – her work hours are quite flexible so she shouldn't have to zip back to Boulder terribly early. When she stays with us, she's got a futon in her old bedroom. But you two would have to share a bathroom."

This is working out better than I expected. I don't think Lacey has any idea that I know about her cancer, so her instinct to avoid talking about difficult topics hasn't yet been triggered. "That's great, Lacey. I've got you plugged into my GPS, so I'll plan to be there by 6:30."

"Come earlier if that's easier for you. The garage code is 4229. Just make yourself at home."

We sign off, agreeing that she'll call her daughter to pass along our plans. Despite that, I decide to give Em a heads-up.

We're on for dinner at your folks' home tonight. She invited me to stay the night & we hope you will too.

Her reply comes in a moment later.

**Awesome!! i'll work on her to take tomorrow off
& i have a personal day coming so no prob.
yea!!!**

Yea, indeed, with lots of exclamation points!

That was the easy part. Now to decide when to broach the cancer topic. Meanwhile, I'd better hit the road.

Chapter 21

"When are you going to talk to Mom about her cancer?" Em whispers as we find ourselves in the kitchen for a moment without Lacey.

I set the stack of dirty dishes on the counter beside the sink. "Soon. Do you want to be there when I do?"

"Not at first," she says, turning on the water to rinse the plates. "She's going to be pissed at me for telling you. Maybe I'll hide out in my room or something."

Oops – here's Lacey with the garlic bread we didn't finish off and the empty salad bowl and tongs. Em and I exchange a quick look. "Soon," I mouth in her direction.

As soon as we finish cleaning up the dinner dishes, Em quietly disappears in the direction of the bedrooms. "Would you like a little ice cream for dessert?" Lacey offers.

I pat my stomach and roll my eyes. "After all that spaghetti, I feel like I may never need to eat again. But if you'd like some, please go ahead." Lacey spent more time moving her food around on her plate than actually eating. I wonder if her cancer treatments are affecting her appetite.

She turns on some background music – light jazz – and we settle on the couch in her living room. When I first arrived, I visited with Lacey in the kitchen as she enhanced the salad from the restaurant and warmed garlic bread in the oven, helping out with odds and ends. Now I can ask her about the photos displayed on the credenza in the living room. She joins me as I examine each picture. A family shot of her and husband Adam with little Em between them, raising her up by her arms so she could "fly." Others depict my granddaughter at various ages, some by herself and some with a parent. Skimming down a water slide at an outdoor pool. Taking a curtain call with classmates when she was nine. Dusted with flour as she bakes with a woman I learn is her paternal grandmother, whom she calls Bibi. A huge thanksgiving gathering on a massive table, which included both sets of grandparents, a middle-aged couple – Adam's sister and her husband – and two young cousins. There's a shot of around a dozen people wearing the hip-length white coats I associate with doctors. Its decorative frame reads "Congratulations Nurse Practitioner Graduates." Adam stands out as the only man in the group, as well as the only African American. Framed pictures hang on the wall above the rest of the display depicting more formal portraits of Sheila and Forrest Linscott, the couple who adopted Lacey; and Celestine and Lionel Blankenship, Adam's parents.

I linger at the photo of the Linscotts, fingering my bracelet as I choose my next words. The jewelry was a gift to me from Lacey and Em the first time we met in person. The corded bracelet holds a silver charm depicting a tree, similar to a tree of life symbol, but with no apparent trunk. Em picked it out because she felt it was symbolic of her family tree, with both adopted and biological connections that spread in many directions. I cherish it.

"I just learned that you lost your parents," I say, turning toward my daughter, who seems deep in thought as she gazes at their portrait. "I'm so sorry, Lacey."

She frowns slightly. "Em must have told you." I nod. She bites her lip. "I'm sorry I never said anything to you. I meant to, but it never seemed like the right time."

"No need to apologize. I just wish I had known so I could have offered some support. A shoulder to lean on."

She sighs, her eyes turned downward. "You know, it's kind of ironic. I lost my father and mother only a year after finding my birth mother." She looks into my eyes. "I was just getting used to the idea of having two moms."

She turns back toward the couch moments after I glimpse the dampness in her eyes. "Lacey," I say, reaching over to rest a hand on her shoulder, "would you like a hug?"

Nodding while pressing her lips tight, she spins back toward me and falls into my embrace. I rub her back as we hold each other, remembering many times when Ruth has comforted me this same way. After just a short while, I realize we are breathing in perfect unison. I wait until she starts to release her grip, then drop one arm but keep the other hand on her shoulder.

"Thanks, Ellie. I needed that." She manages a weak smile, but it expands as I smile back.

We sit again and she wonders out loud what has become of her daughter. "She used to spend hours on the phone with her friends after dinner, but that was back in high school."

"I remember doing the same thing at that age," I say. "Of course, back then we had a landline with one of those curly cords, and I'd stretch it out from the kitchen wall and sit at the top of the stairs to the basement to try to have some privacy."

Her face lights up. "We had a cordless phone, but you couldn't take the handset very far from its base or you'd lose the call. I knew all the best spots in the house where I could still talk and not have the sound be all garbled."

I adjust my position so I can look more directly at her. "I suppose our parents were just as amused about things we did like that as you and Adam are with what Em did growing up."

"I'm sure they were. I certainly gave them plenty to be amused about. And some things that they didn't find amusing in the least." I can read in her eyes that she's remembering times when she was growing up. Stories she'll think to share with me, and many I'll never hear.

If her parents were here – the real ones who raised her, rather than myself and a long-ago teenaged boyfriend – would she have kept her cancer diagnosis a secret? If her mother had then found out, what might she have said or done?

Well, that mother isn't here, but I am. I don't have any experience at being a mom, but I know how to be a friend. Keeping this secret can't be good for Lacey or for her husband and daughter who love her.

"Lacey, I know you've been dealing with a difficult situation and haven't reached out to the people closest to you for support."

Her eyes open wide for a moment before she gathers her thoughts. "You mean when my folks passed away..."

"No. I'm talking about you and your health."

"Em told you," she says, scowling.

"Yes, she did," I say, scooting closer to her and reaching out a hand for hers. She hesitates, but takes it. "Don't be upset with her, Lacey. She's concerned about you and wants to be supportive. She believes that you've kept your diagnosis and treatment secret from her father as well. Is that true?"

Lacey stares at our hands, then nods.

"You have cancer?" I say, my voice as gentle as I can make it.

"Yes. Cervical. I'm ..." she hesitates, trying to maintain control. "I'm undergoing concurrent chemo-radiation – both chemo and radiation together."

"How long will that continue?"

168

"Four more weeks. I just started last week. That's why I said at first that I couldn't see you other than over the weekend. I go in to the cancer center every weekday. That's where I was before coming home tonight."

"And then what happens? How soon will you know if the treatment is working?"

She shrugs. "Weeks, maybe months. My oncologist says it can vary a lot. We'll just have to wait and see how the tests look."

I'm afraid to ask my next question, but feel I must know. Em and Adam will surely want to know. "What are they saying about your chances for it going into remission?"

She swallows hard. "They caught it pretty early. Not super early, but not too bad. Dr. Singh told me that over 90% of cases like mine survive at least five years."

I nod encouragingly. "Ninety percent! That's good!"

Lacey looks away and tears spill from her eyes. "So, one out of ten people die within five years. And who knows how many more die in six or seven or ..." She pulls her hand free from mine. "I'm not even quite 50 yet! I'm not ready to ..."

I close the gap between us and take her in my arms. "I know," I whisper, rocking her. I draw on all my courage to remain strong, to not break down myself. Lacey needs me. "I know it's scary."

When I hear her breathing steady, I sit back and hold her face gently between my hands. "It's going to work out all right," I say. "No matter what happens, focus on the love and the beauty in your life. Find the joy when you and Adam get up every morning to share a new day. Relish the love you and Em have for each other. Rejoice in the wonders of the world around you."

We sit still, our eyes taking each other in. In so many ways, I feel like I am looking at myself at a slightly younger age. Life can feel like it is tearing us apart, but comfort can be found both within ourselves and with the help of people who care about us. Joy may come from the smallest places, but we may have to search for it.

Lacey's expression softens and her mouth begins to turn into a tiny smile. "I'm glad we found each other. You've said you don't know what kind of a mother you could have been. I think you're a wonderful mother, and a very special friend."

Now it's my turn to cry, but I'm smiling so much my cheeks ache.

When I arrived early this evening, I questioned whether the earrings I had chosen for my daughter would be appropriate, not knowing just what her cancer prognosis might be. I choose to take the path of optimism and hope. Retrieving my small handbag, I extract the delicate interlinked hoops and hand them to her. "For you."

She stares at the sentiment printed on the card, sniffs once, but then reads it out loud. "'Here's to the wonderful memories we have yet to make together.'" She bites her lip, blinking rapidly, then reaches out for another hug. "They're perfect, Ellie. Thank you so much."

She removes her simple studs and replaces them with the new earrings. "They look lovely on you," I say.

"Would you like to visit the Botanic Gardens tomorrow?" she says, perking up. "I just have one article to wrap up and submit in the morning, but I'm sure I can finish that off by 10:00."

"I'd love that. Do you think there's any chance Em can join us, like we originally planned?"

"I'll bet she can pull it off. Like me, she works remotely and has very flexible hours. I'll check with her. But first," she says, pecking me on the cheek as she stands, "Em and I need to have an important talk. You've set the bar really high, you know!"

"You're up to the challenge, Lacey," I say as she walks down the hallway toward her daughter's room.

Chapter 22

It's a glorious warm day with a spectacularly blue sky – perfect for strolling through the varied garden displays. It's a good thing Em got online last night to buy tickets – they were nearly sold out.

I remember visiting the Denver Botanic Gardens once or twice back when I was growing up here. The iconic arched, lattice-like greenhouse is still here. I remember how fun it was when my friends and I spotted its structure in the old *Sleeper* movie, along with the "spaceship" house along Interstate 70, and the "ski-jump" church on South Monaco. Oddly, I don't remember there being much a garden outside of the original building back then. Now, the gardens span twenty-four acres!

At my request, we start with the greenhouse, which is filled with tropical plants and more humidity than Denver ever experiences. Em is antsy to visit the various water gardens, so we move outdoors and follow a pathway toward the largest of them, but there are so many delightful displays along the way that we keep wandering down side paths. A hundred shades of green show off flowers of yellow and purple and scarlet. Hundreds of evergreens and deciduous trees – some familiar, but many I don't recall ever seeing before – shade us from the increasing heat of the sun.

Colorful sculptures bring even more visual variety to the displays.

"I need to sit," Lacey says, sinking onto a bench under a shade structure. We join her, mesmerized by the floating water lilies with pink blossoms and the tall grasses that seem to be growing right out of the pond across from us.

"You doing okay, Mom? Em takes her hand.

She nods. "I thought the treatments weren't affecting how I feel, but I may have been premature in thinking that."

"Do you want to head back?" I ask.

"No, no. I just need a few minutes. Then, maybe we can grab some lunch?"

I'm glad to hear that she's thinking about food, although her suggestion could be more about extra time to sit and rest than being hungry. Em studies the facility map and discovers that there is an onsite Bistro close by.

We find another lovely shaded spot to enjoy our lunches close to a garden focused on native plants that Lacey seems especially interested in. "I'd love to pick up some ideas for my own yard," she explains. "We'd like to take out the rest of the grass in the back yard and put in more flowers and ground cover that can do well in our dry climate."

As we eat, a small group stops nearby to focus on the area that we're facing. A slender, blond woman who I'd guess is in her forties seems to be showing off the gardens to a couple of visiting friends, judging by their easy laughter and taking of selfies of the three of them.

"Michelle," the man says, leaning over and pointing at a plant of interest, "what's this one?"

The blond – Michelle – crouches beside him and declares, "That's *Amsonia jonesii* or Jones' Bluestar." She goes on to describe in great detail where this particular flower grows, how common it is, and a number of other details that leave me with my mouth hanging open.

"And this one?" the dark-haired woman asks. Again Michelle rattles off an encyclopedic answer, complete with tongue-twisting Latin words, the common name – some sort of aster – and she points out several other little yellow flowers that are also asters, but have somewhat different names.

By this time, Lacey has risen to her feet and is creeping closer to Michelle and friends, fascinated by her obvious expertise. Em and I gather up our empty sandwich wrappers to join her. I'm disappointed to notice that Lacey still has half her lunch in her brown bag. I thought she had managed to finish everything. Maybe she'll want more later.

Michelle notices us standing nearby, obviously listening to her explanations of what's growing before us. "Hi," she says, smiling at us with the same enthusiasm as she's been showing her friends. "Are you enjoying the gardens?"

"Very much," Lacey answers. "And I'm sorry to intrude, but we couldn't help but be impressed with how knowledgeable you are. Do you work here?"

She laughs, her eyes sparkling. "I do, but I'm usually hidden away in a lab or out doing studies in the field. I'm just showing my out-of-town friends around today."

"On her day off, no less," the man says. "We get our very own scientist to try to stump."

The woman pipes in. "So far, Michelle's known every single plant."

Michelle laughs, pointing vaguely toward plants at the back of the display. "*Omnino leviculus.*"

"Which one is … *omnino* whatever?" I ask. "And what's the common name? I can never remember the Latin."

She grins at us. "*Omnino leviculus* means *Absolutely clueless,* or something close to that. See, the cool thing is, I can make up Latin-sounding names if I don't know one." We all laugh and try making up words that sound vaguely Latin.

"Rootitooti Anthillitchia."

"Prius Onomatopoeia."

"Rediculus Michellennium."

"Who are you calling ridiculous?" Michelle laughs.

We're having such a lovely time talking to this group that I miss noticing the color drain from Lacey's face. She grabs hold of her daughter's arm, looking terrible shaky.

"Please excuse us," I say hurriedly as I take Lacey's other arm and help Em walk her back to our bench.

"Are you okay?" Michelle asks, following us. "Is there anything I can do to help?"

Lacey sips at a bottle of water Em hands her, then waves her hand dismissively. "I'm fine. Maybe just a little overheated."

Realizing that Lacey probably doesn't want any more of a fuss than we've already caused, I thank Michelle and her friends. "Thank you for your concern. We're good. Please, go ahead and enjoy your tour."

They move away, glancing back at us now and then to check on how Lacey is doing. She manages a weak smile and a wave. "I'm feeling better now, girls, but I think I'm done for the day. How about we start making our way back?"

We make frequent stops as we navigate back to the entrance. Lacey seems fatigued, but I don't get the impression, like I did before, that she might collapse. Em latches onto her arm whenever we're on the move. Finally back at the car, Em insists on taking the wheel, encouraging her mother to tilt the passenger seat way back and relax. I like the fact that I can easily see her face from my spot in the back seat. Minutes after pulling out of the parking lot, Lacey is asleep.

***

"Frankly, it's not as bad as I had feared," I tell Ruth, speaking quietly on the phone so others can't hear. "I was imagining an advanced cancer; something untreatable. You know how I can work myself up worrying." I stroll through Lacey's back yard over to a circular plot of tea roses and lean over to inhale the fragrance of a deep, red bloom.

"Yes, dear, I do know. I'm relieved to hear that her chances are good, and also that she's got people to talk to about it now."

"She couldn't have kept it a secret much longer anyway – not with the side effects of her chemo and radiation therapy. So far, she's just been fatigued and has no appetite. That could change. She put off telling Adam because she was afraid he'd cancel his trip to the nursing conference if he knew beforehand, but she promised to talk to him once he gets home Thursday."

Our conversation turns to an update on news of Ruth and her family. She had a noneventful and leisurely drive to northern Colorado and is settled into the new campground – the one we intended to meet at yesterday. "It's lovely," she reports. "We can see a lake from our sites."

Carol and Nick left early this morning to head back home to San Diego. "They're taking a few extra days to make the trip. It sounds like their bosses were both quite understanding about what they'd been through, so they don't have to show up at work until next week."

"I would hope so. They've each been at their same companies for decades, right?"

"True, but nowadays, loyalty to your employer doesn't always mean the employer will be loyal back. They're both lucky, I guess."

Lucky, indeed, and for reasons unrelated to sympathetic managers. When I left, they could hardly stand it if they weren't holding hands every moment. Their previous disagreements were forgotten – at least for a while. I wonder what effect this scare will have on them as time passes.

"What are your plans, dear? Have you decided how long you'll stay with your daughter?"

I feel torn. Lacey and I discussed my plans earlier this evening, and she encouraged me to continue with my trip. "Ellie, having you here these couple of days was exactly what I needed. You helped me realize that I needed to open up to Em and allow her to support me. She's an adult now, and strange as it feels to recognize that, it's also extremely heartening to realize that she's grown up to be a strong, caring woman."

"You and Adam deserve a lot of credit for how your child has turned out."

With Adam due home on Thursday, Lacey convinced me that she has her nearby support network covered. "We can still talk by phone." I promised to call regularly. How could I possibly not?

I tell Ruth that I'll be arriving by dinnertime tomorrow, and her excitement helps me recognize how much I'm looking forward to camping with her again and to resume our joint adventures.

"That's wonderful news, dear! I've been holding off on that long hike we thought sounded so gorgeous. Do you feel up to tackling it your first full day here?"

She's going to run me into the ground, but I realize I'm beaming at the thought of sharing the adventure with her. "You bet! See you soon."

Chapter 23

"I need to take this," I tell Lacey when I read the caller ID on my phone's screen. It's Agent Edgar Garcia from the Colorado Bureau of Investigation. I've been so wrapped up with the search for Carol and dealing with my daughter's cancer diagnosis that I'd completely put the camera mystery out of my thoughts.

I scurry back indoors, leaving Lacey lounging under the awning of her back porch, sipping at an iced tea. We had considered visiting a museum or window-shopping along the 16th Street Mall downtown, but she clearly didn't have the energy for any of that.

Agent Garcia repeats several of the same questions he asked me the first time we talked. I describe how a glint of light caught my eye and what the terrain was like where the camera was found.

"The photo you first sent of the man standing at the overlook," he says, "You thought you recognized that setting. How certain are you of that?"

"I'm completely certain," I reply. "Ruth and I stopped at that same spot and I took a picture of her there."

He asks me to send him that photo and I promise to take care of it as soon as we finish our call. I re-confirm that we were hiking the Sidestep Trail. "Did you receive the file I sent from my GPS tracking app?" I say. "I marked the approximate spots on that map where we found the camera and where that overlook was."

"Yes, that was helpful."

I would think it was *extremely* helpful. It seems like he could be a bit more enthusiastic about what we discovered, but maybe I'm imagining that this "evidence" is much more important than it really is. I've been picturing myself as a clever Miss Marple, but perhaps I'm more of a clueless Stephanie Plum. Or the Pink Panther's bumbling Inspector Clouseau.

Before he ends our conversation, I decide to plunge in and ask my question. "I've heard from people who've seen the photos that they think the shots are of Aurora and Blake Zakarian. And that Aurora went missing about three years ago. Does that match up with what you're looking at?"

The agent hesitates a beat before answering. "I can't confirm that we've positively identified the people in the photos. But I can tell you that if that turns out to be correct, we will be re-opening the Zakarian case."

Good. Figuring he can't be any more specific than that, I resist telling him more of my own theory. If they're looking at the cold case, they'll surely hone in on the discrepancies between Blake Zakarian's story of his wife's disappearance and what's in those pictures.

As soon as we hang up, I scroll through my phone's memory for the photo of Ruth at the overlook. I attach it to an email, along with a shot I took of the wildflower meadow that nearly matched an image on the old camera. I include a note explaining both pictures, then add, "Please let me know if these lead to learning what happened to Aurora Zakarian."

Shortly after I send my message, Agent Garcia responds. "Photos received. Thank you for your assistance."

Nothing about keeping me in the loop. Oh well – I tried.

***

Lacey and I spend the rest of the morning talking about happy memories in each of our lives, getting to know each other's history better, and discovering odds and ends we have in common. We're surprised to learn that we've both visited the Bucksnort Saloon in Sphinx Park, Colorado. "It's still in existence?" I ask, calculating that I was last there nearly fifty years ago with a carload of friends enjoying a day in the mountains. I ate an enormous hamburger and proudly ordered my first legal beer.

We share stories of favorite schoolteachers and subjects. "Mrs. Emerson – 9th grade English!" she declares and I come back with "Mrs. Kniss – 8th grade English!" Our parallel careers may have been shaped by those classes. First dates and college roommates, best-loved ice cream treats and fantastic concert seats – so many special memories.

My departure from my daughter's place feels hopeful rather than tearful. We hug and kiss each other's cheeks. "Text me when you get there," she says as I climb into my SUV.

"I will. Oh! I almost forgot these!" I say, realizing I'd left Em's gift – wild-colored socks – on the passenger seat. "I hope Em likes them."

Lacey peeks inside the bag. "She'll love them, Ellie. I'll give them to her when she comes back down to visit this weekend."

We trade a few more departing notes – *Drive safely* – *Take care of yourself* – and I finally start the engine and pull away, waving as I leave.

In my entire life, has it ever before been this hard to say goodbye? There's a lump in my throat as I navigate my way toward the main highway I'll be taking toward Grand Lake west of Rocky Mountain National Park. *She'll beat this*, I repeat to myself. *Stay positive.*

Colorado's mountain scenery is breath-taking. Every part of the Rocky Mountain range seems to have its own character. The route I've chosen climbs steeply through numerous switch-backs, but my vehicle's powerful engine is more than adequate for towing my A-frame camper, which is locked down into a boxy shape that rides lower than the height of the Xterra. The highway seems much safer than I remember from my youth – reassuring guardrails whenever the drop-off is steep and a second lane for the uphill climb, which I appreciate because I tend to drive below the speed limit while pulling a trailer, especially through sharp curves.

Chuckling, I remember my dad cursing out the trucks for driving so slowly up to this pass. Back then, I'm not sure there were any opportunities to get around them. It drove him crazy, but I enjoyed being able to peer into the shadows of the Engelmann spruce and lodgepole pine trees, searching for deer or even chipmunks or snowshoe hares, since we had sometimes spotted animals from the car just before they disappeared into the woods.

I notice patches of snow remaining on the slopes above the top of the mountain pass, but then the road descends rapidly through more switch-backs, finally straightening out in a high mountain valley. I pass the entrance to a ski area, its slopes green and totally devoid of snow. The rest of my drive will be smooth sailing.

The large lakes in this region shouldn't be much farther away, but I've yet to spot them. My GPS announces that my turn off the U.S. highway onto a graded gravel road is coming up, so I accept that Ruth and I may need to drive further north to visit Lake Granby and Grand Lake. It's going to be so wonderful to see her again, and I'm excited about the hikes we've picked out. We don't have the full two weeks we originally planned, but still have plenty of time to explore the area.

Moments after I pull into my campsite, she and Charli are here to greet me. Ruth looks herself again – the stress of this past weekend has disappeared from her face. Charli rubs against my legs until I reach down to run my fingers along her back. That goal achieved, she starts batting around a pine cone, sending it flying beneath my car, then launching it toward Ruth and me.

"Have you been giving her catnip?" I ask, laughing at her high-energy antics. "You'd think she was a kitten again."

"Second childhood," Ruth answers, "Kind of like me."

It feels so good to have Ruth back to her usual self. She helps me raise the main walls of my camper to form the A-shape and I step inside to lift the triangular side walls and lock them in place. As I finish my usual camp set-up tasks, Ruth asks about Lacey's mood when I left.

"I think it's been a great relief for her to share her secret with Em and me, and I expect it'll be even better once Adam gets home tomorrow and she confides in him. I told her, and I'm sure her doctors have as well, that it's important to find ways to reduce stress and welcome support from the people who love her."

"This isn't something she should try to handle all on her own. You did the right thing, dear, insisting on seeing her after Carol's debacle sidetracked your plans."

If I had been the mother who raised her, there would never have been a moment's thought before making that trip to Denver. Nothing will change our history, but we can shape our present and future. Smiling, I say, "I'm very glad I went. I've seen how you are with your daughters. I'm learning from *you*."

"I think you simply have a big heart and the instinct to follow it."

This calls for an embrace. One of the things I love about

my friendship with Ruth is that she's a big hugger. Not that I was aloof or untouchable before meeting her, but my daily hug count has probably quadrupled from its previous record since she came into my life. And they say hugs are good for our health. I prolong our embrace and she shows no signs of breaking it off until I'm ready.

"Ahhhhh," we breath in unison.

Now that my endorphins are joyously dancing through my body, I accept Ruth's invitation to take in my new surroundings. "I waited for you to get here before exploring the lake," she says. She's referring to the small body of water adjoining our campground. You won't see motorboats and speedboats, sailboats and jet skis on this little beauty, but we don't have the crowds either. She estimates the entire circumference can be traversed in under an hour, so she brings the cat backpack out. Charli wastes no time crawling into it, clearly understanding that an adventure is about to begin. This time, Ruth swings the pack up onto her back without assistance. "I think Charli likes the sense of flying," she says. The cat is purring at full volume. It sounds like Ruth is wearing a jet-pack and may take off at any moment.

"Ready for launch?" she says, and I burst out laughing. Sometimes we're so attuned to each other that I swear she reads my mind.

Our little lake is surrounded by dense forest and is sparkling in the afternoon sunlight. There's a well-trodden path circling it, and we soon pass a couple with two young children heading in the opposite direction. Looking beyond the far end of the lake, we see a towering peak, steep rock walls drawing the eye up to a rounded summit. I pull out my phone to take a photo, then zoom in to emphasize the distant mountain.

"What's that in the water?" Ruth asks, pointing to a spot slightly closer to us. "A boulder?"

I can't make it out any better than she can, but I take a

shot of the dark object and expand its display. I still can't identify it. We continue walking, and I squint at the thing every now and then as we draw closer.

"It's a moose!" I'm quite excited – I've never seen a moose in the wild before. "I think we'll be able to see it better after we pass these bushes."

As I'd hoped, our new vantage point offers a clear view of the large animal. No antlers, so it's a female. I'd love to see her up close and wonder if it would be safe for us to proceed along the lake shore, which looks like it may take us within a stone's throw of the moose as she dunks her face in the water, browsing for grasses and other plants growing from the bottom.

"I think we can get a bit closer without upsetting her," Ruth says, and we proceed slowly and silently until we're about a hundred yards away. The creature either hasn't noticed us or simply doesn't care about a couple of insignificant little humans. She's bigger than a horse.

"Maybe it would be better if we make a *little* noise," Ruth whispers. "We don't want to startle her."

I'm a bit nervous about getting any closer, but I decide we can watch for her reaction once she knows we're here. "Okay," I say in a normal voice.

"Okay, then," she echoes. The moose lifts her head and turns to look over her shoulder in the opposite direction of where we're standing.

"Maybe our voices echoed," I suggest. We move forward in slow motion.

"Hello, moose. We're just passing by," Ruth says in a calming tone of voice.

"Don't mind us," I add.

"We're just a couple of ladies out for a stroll." When I don't say anything, she turns back toward me. "Keep talking. We want her to know there are two of us."

The cat meows and I can see her staring in fascination at the enormous critter. She doesn't seem distressed – only curious. So far.

"Make that three of us," Ruth says, continuing forward.

"Are you sure this is a good idea?"

It's at that moment that I spot another hiker just beyond the moose. She's far closer to it than we are and is engrossed in taking photos of the animal. That's what the moose was looking at.

Before I can say a word, the creature lifts her head again, now staring at the woman, whose focus has shifted to something on the shore, hidden from our view by a clump of shrubs. She takes a few steps in that direction and the moose suddenly springs from the water, aiming straight for the hiker.

"Look out!" I scream as the animal thrusts her front legs at the woman, who falls to the ground. The moose steps back and is joined a moment later by two calves with impossibly long legs. She leads her babies away from the lake and into the woods.

Ruth is already running toward the slumped figure on the ground and I follow, trying not to stumble on rocks or roots that make the footing uneven.

"It tried to kick me," the woman is saying as I arrive, panting hard. "I thought it would trample me!"

"Thank goodness she only warned you off," Ruth says. "Come on. Let's move away from here before she changes her mind."

We help her to her feet, but she resists leaving before picking up her phone off the ground. "Oh no! The screen is cracked!"

"Let's go before one of our heads gets cracked," Ruth insists, one hand placed on the lady's back as she physically encourages her to hurry. Looking back over my shoulder at the spot where the moose family disappeared into the woods, I wave impatiently, hurrying them along. Let's go!

Finally in motion, we hurry a few hundred yards before stopping to catch our breath. "Are you doing all right?" Ruth asks.

She nods, checking herself over. "Looks like I scraped my elbow a bit and maybe my shoulder, but I'm okay. If I hadn't stumbled over backwards, I think she would have caught me in the stomach. I'm more freaked out than hurt. Thank you for chasing it away."

More like the moose decided her message had been sent and received. Ruth tactfully but emphatically lectures the woman on keeping her distance from wildlife. "You were lucky. If her hooves had hit you, we wouldn't be standing here having this conversation."

Her expression somber, she nods. Message received.

"Are you staying at the campground?" Ruth asks.

"Yes. I'm here with my mom," she replies. "She's back at our camper sitting and enjoying the scenery. I wanted to bring her back photos of the moose and its babies. She doesn't hike, but she loves nature and wildlife." She introduces herself as Melody. Her mother is Mona. We tell her our names, including presenting our kitty companion to her. She's charmed by the cat's comfort at being toted around in a pack. Charli doesn't even seem fazed by the mad dash Ruth made minutes ago or the defensive mama moose.

I've seen folks who sit around outside their campers all day long, and I'm always curious what they do with their time if they don't hike or at least take short walks, especially if they are nowhere near "civilization." I ask, "Your mom doesn't enjoy hiking?" The entire loop is only about a mile, and I'm guessing Melody was merely a quarter mile into it when she encountered the moose.

Melody shrugs. "She used to love hiking, but now she says she's too old. It's too bad. She's still up for taking walks on the paved bike paths near her home, but actual dirt trails? Forget it."

Ruth and I exchange glances. Too old? It sounds like she's still physically capable of hiking. I can't resist asking how old her mother is, since Melody seems to be only in her thirties.

"She's 65," she replies. "She just started on Medicare."

"Huh," I say. "She and I are the same age. And Ruth is ... well, go ahead and guess how old she is."

"Oh, I'm terrible at ages," she says, looking closely at Ruth's face, her trim build, and her neon yellow shirt and rainbow-colored ball cap. "Maybe 70?" she says, her eyes shifting from my face to Ruth's. I have a feeling she would have guessed lower, but already figured out that I must be younger than my friend because of how I worded my question.

"Try 85," I announce with pride, as if I had anything to do with Ruth's remarkable vigor and fitness.

"Not for another two months," Ruth adds.

"No. Way." Her eyes open wide in amazement.

I love when this happens. Maybe when we meet Mona and she sees what two senior ladies are up to, she may decide that gives her permission to take up hiking again.

Chapter 24

Our long hike yesterday more than lived up to our expectations. Views of the various lakes in the region were awe-inspiring, the air was rich with the scent of pine, the high peaks rugged and gorgeous with patches of snow contrasting with the deep cerulean sky. But it wore me out. Back at camp, I showered, then decided to lie down for a few minutes to rest my eyes. When they popped open again, I realized that I'd been out for nearly an hour.

Today, I get a break. We'll tackle Trail Ridge Road by car, following the paved road as it climbs some 4,000 feet, crossing over a mountain range. Although I imagine my parents drove it with me at some time in my childhood, I really don't recall any details of that excursion. I insist on driving, having heard that some of the route is curvy and skirts dramatic drop-offs. With that being the case, I prefer being the one to decide how much to slow down and how far to squeeze away from the edge of the road.

We pack some snacks and water, hoping to find a scenic spot where we can enjoy a bite. We might even hike a short way to a lookout point.

The famous road starts climbing out of the valley fairly quickly, and soon we reach the first of many, many hairpin curves taking us higher and higher. Forest and rocky outcroppings predominate, with low stone walls instead of guard rails providing some comfort in the places where the slope drops off more steeply to our right. We climb, and climb some more, navigating turn after turn. On the brief straightaways, I snatch a glance at the peaks across from us and I'm aware of how deep the valley below us seems. Actually, we can no longer see all the way to the bottom.

"There's a pull-out just ahead," Ruth points out. "Stop so you can enjoy the views, too."

When we emerge from the car, the change in temperature at this altitude is already noticeable. I reach back inside and slip on a light windbreaker.

"I wonder how many miles away those mountains are?" Ruth says, pointing across the valley.

"I'm guessing the closer ones are under five miles, but those snowy ones beyond them? Maybe ten miles? Twenty?" Truthfully, I'm terrible at estimating distances like these.

We take a few shots, including a selfie angled so the camera is pointing down into the valley, then resume our drive. More curves, more climbing, and the terrain is starting to change. We pass a sign noting that we are passing 10,000 feet elevation. The trees are becoming shorter and look more tortured by the elements, until they disappear entirely. We're now above treeline, where nothing seems to grow, except for green splotches of grass-like plants huddling amidst groupings of small rocks. The distant views, no longer hidden by forests, become even more stunning.

At a small parking area near 12,000 feet, we stop. Putting on warmer jackets, we decide to follow a paved path that promises to teach us more about our tundra surroundings. On foot, we're able to see that the patches of vegetation aren't all identical. Tiny yellow blooms erupt from some, while blues and lavenders decorate other spots. Some of the flowers seem far too fragile to exist in this harsh environment, which can be covered with dozens of feet of snow in the winter. Even now, a toasty-warm July day in the valleys, it's about 50° F and breezy up here. We pick up our pace so we can warm up.

"Look at these!" Ruth says as a cluster of crazy-shaped rocks come into view, breaking up the relative monotony of the terrain immediately surrounding us. "Let's take a look."

She's hiking at her usual, swift clip over toward a rock formation that reminds me of a shiitake mushroom on a tall stem. I'm panting like I just completed a marathon and feel slightly light-headed. This altitude! "I'll just wait for you here," I manage to holler. She waves in acknowledgement and I watch as she weaves among the rocks, scrambling up onto one that resembles a large throne and sitting briefly, waving one hand at me in a regal manner. Queen of the mushroom rocks.

When she returns to join me on the main path, I've had time to catch my breath, so we forge onward to the end of the trail where larger and even more fanciful rock formations lie. Along with other tourists, we wind our way among the natural structures, wondering at the brilliant yellow and orange lichen adding splashes of color to the rocks. Tenacious ground cover plants squeeze into cracks and gaps, and rugged openings between the formations frame dramatic views of mountains in the distance. A broad swatch of snow still clings to a north-facing slope just below us. Photo op!

We tuck ourselves into a sheltering spot out of the breeze and take time to eat our energy bars and drink some water. My head aches, but this break seems to be helping it improve.

"Ready to move on?" Ruth asks, stuffing her trash in her pocket.

"Onward and downward," I say, rising awkwardly to my feet and waiting a moment to regain my equilibrium. I'm definitely ready for downward.

We continue driving east, eventually dropping down into Estes Park, a charming yet incredibly congested little mountain town. My headache has disappeared and my energy level is back to normal.

Although it would be much shorter to simply reverse course and drive the high road back over the mountains the way we came, we opt for a lower route that circles around and eventually lands us in the Grand Lake area. This time, we're viewing some of the same terrain from the valleys rather than from above. Now that it's afternoon, the traffic has increased considerably. Ruth offers to take over driving at a scenic pullout, and I'm happy to let her. No more steep drop-offs from this stage on, as far as I can tell.

We're both famished by the time we roll back into camp. No wonder – all we've eaten since breakfast were a couple of energy bars. "Let's order take-out," I suggest and retrieve my laptop to peruse restaurant choices.

"It'll be much more peaceful eating it here in camp," she says before driving off to pick up our order.

While she's gone, I send a quick note to my daughter, offering encouragement. Adam's flight should have landed a little while ago. I wonder if she'll tell him tonight, or wait until morning to give him a chance to unwind before slamming him with such troubling news. I search recent news articles for any mention of the name Zakarian. Nothing. Of course, the agent with the Colorado Bureau of Investigation hasn't even had the camera and memory card for a full week yet. Patience is not one of my virtues.

Instead, I scroll through old postings about Aurora Zakarian's disappearance. Clicking on a video clip from a news conference shortly after she was reported missing, I study her husband's face carefully as he looks into the camera and pleads with his audience, *Please, if you know anything about what happened to Aurora, let someone know.* He appears to be distraught, but he could also be a good actor.

One article I hadn't come across earlier offers some details which are new to me. Blake Zakarian's alibi for the day his wife disappeared was that he spent the day with his brother, Isaak. Blake and Isaak Zakarian – their parents must have loved that "k" sound.

Blake claimed that his wife had gone hiking alone – that much I knew. It was his brother, Isaak, who drove him to the Little Brook trailhead after Aurora didn't return home by dark. After finding her car parked there – the only vehicle in the lot – they hiked up the trail a ways, searching for her, before Blake sent his brother to drive until he found cell coverage and called 9-1-1.

A chill runs up my spine. This scene feels far too close to our own recent ordeal.

Could Blake and his brother have come up with this story to cover up what really happened to Aurora? If she and Blake had been hiking on the Sidestep trail that day, as the camera indicated, then how did her car end up at a different trailhead?

I pull up the best photos showing Blake and Aurora's faces. Then I watch the interview again. Wait – I just realized he's clean-shaven in the video. No goatee. I freeze the frame and zoom in on his face in the still photo. I think that's the same person, but now I'm not 100% sure. The only shot of Aurora that I found on the camera was from a few years earlier. I compare that to the only photo every article seems to show of her. Again, certainly a strong resemblance, but a tiny doubt has crept into my mind. Those people on the hiking forum who identified the pictures as being the Zakarians – how sure were they? Have I been so intrigued with solving a mystery that I was willing to talk myself into any sort of startling theory?

Another uncertainty occurs to me. Those older cameras didn't access the current date from the internet. You had to manually set the date. If you changed the batteries, I think you lost the date and time and had to enter them again.

Suppose that Superman and Lois Lane actually are the Zakarians. But, what if the date on the final batch of pictures on that old camera was wrong? Maybe it was simply a crazy coincidence that they were saved to the camera's memory card with the same date as when Aurora disappeared. The Zakarians could have taken that hike together the previous week or the previous summer.

And here I thought Ruth and I had cracked open a cold case. Maybe we need to crack open a cold case of white wine. That may be as close as we get. No wonder Agent Garcia sounded so noncommittal on the phone. He probably thinks we're a couple of crazy old ladies with too much time on our hands and far too vivid imaginations.

Chapter 25

"We can go tubing!" Ruth says, waving her phone while pointing at it with her other hand.

She's always up for a new adventure. "Whitewater tubing? I don't think I'm up for that. Unless the river is really gentle."

"No, not in water. On a hillside. Like sledding in the winter, but on inner tubes. Look at this."

She holds her screen out for me to see. From this vantage point, the image seems to show a couple of people sitting in brightly-colored, circular sleds, sliding down a snowy hill. I think Ruth has gone daffy. There's nearly no snow left in the mountains this time of year. Yet, when I reach for the phone and bring it closer, I realize there's a swath of green just beyond the white ground. And the woman on the blue tube is wearing shorts and flip-flops on her feet, while the small child on the green tube has on short sleeves and a helmet that seems bigger than she is. I swipe left to view additional shots, and now realize that the hillside is covered with a distinctly artificial wide stripe of pure white.

"Are they sledding on plastic?" I ask.

"No idea, but it seems to be as slippery as snow. It looks like a blast! I'll bet you must have gone sledding as a girl, growing up in Denver."

"Sure. A few times. There was a park near our house with a small hill, and we used to sled there when there was enough snow on the ground on a weekend, when we didn't have school." Frankly, I don't remember a huge number of times when those two requirements aligned. Like many people who live elsewhere, Ruth may not realize how often Denver's lawns lie bare and brown over the winter, no matter how many feet of snow await skiers in the mountains.

"I seldom got to go sledding as a girl, but the few times I did, I loved it. How about it, dear? Shall I call to reserve a time?"

I suppose if that little kid in the picture can do it, so can I. Although she had her mother hanging onto her tube as they slid down in tandem. Maybe Ruth will do the same for me if it seems too steep.

We pick out a few short trails to explore after our appointed timeslot, and drive to the summertime tubing facility. After receiving some general safety instructions, we pick our colors of sledding tubes. Ruth, with her affinity for bright colors, manages to snatch up one of the rainbow-striped ones that's just been returned. I'm content with a red one, figuring it's the most visible of all so the staff can quickly come to my aid if I crash.

With a conveyor helping us transport our sleds to the top of the hill, I don't have a great deal of time to fret about the steepness of portions of the white descent route. Ruth is easily the oldest in line, and I'm likely second oldest. There are a few teens, but mostly younger children accompanied by an adult, and those parents look to be in their thirties, tops.

I watch carefully as an attendant directs the father and child in front of us to set down their tubes at the summit of the artificial snow. "Forward, backward, or spin?" the young woman asks the kid, who insists that he wants to slide down solo. Dad can wait his turn.

"Backward!" he declares, and the employee rotates him

as instructed, then shoves him down the hill. The boy shrieks in delight.

"Spin," the father says, and the attendant sends him whirling off in a dizzying descent. "Woo hoo!" the man shouts, pumping one fist in the air.

Ruth's smile fills her face. "Come on, Ellie. We're next!"

"I don't know if I..."

She grabs my free hand and drags me and her tube over to the young woman running the show. "My friend is a little nervous," she whispers, not wanting everyone waiting in line behind us to hear.

"No problem. I'll start you off more slowly and facing downhill. Which of you wants to go first?"

I point at Ruth immediately. She settles gracefully onto her tube, still beaming. "Forward this time," she says before being asked, "but I might try spinning on my next ride."

Off she goes, hollering "Whee!" the entire way down. My palms are sweating.

"See how much fun your friend is having? You'll be fine."

Easy for you to say. I back up to my red tube as instructed, looking behind me to make sure I've got it centered before I plop my seat down in the center. It wasn't graceful, but I'm here.

"Forward," I say. "No spinning."

"Got it. Nice and easy, okay?"

Before I can change my mind, I feel a gentle shove and I'm off and sliding. The white slope isn't all one angle – almost immediately, I zip down a steeper section, picking up speed. My tube absorbs the impact as it bounces through the next few dips and rises. Someone is screaming, but I realize that someone is me. I clamp my mouth shut and try not to whimper. Before I know it, I'm at the bottom of the hill, slowing as the terrain flattens and even rises slightly as my tube and I glide toward the padded end of the slippery surface. When I come to a full stop, Ruth is there to lend me a hand to extract myself from my red plastic donut.

"Wasn't that fun?! Come on. Let's get back in line and do it again."

Actually, it *was* fun once I overcame my terror. Still, I'm sticking with "forward" for my next ride. That was exciting enough for me.

Ruth, of course, chooses the other launch options for her next two rides, and opts for both spinning and keeping her eyes closed for her finale. I sled facing forward each time and take pride in my improvement on both settling down into the tube and rolling out of it at the bottom so I can push myself to my feet without assistance. She has her small victories and I have mine.

"That was wonderful, Ellie. I think I got a great video of you."

Please let it be from my most recent ride. Smiling is a much better look on me than screaming in terror.

Afterwards, after turning in our tubes and helmets, we spot a slightly older couple with a pair of children whom we guess to be their grandkids. When I say *slightly older*, I'm still estimating them to be a decade younger than I am, making them about thirty years younger than Ruth. Always comfortable striking up conversations with strangers, Ruth walks over to chat and I follow.

"Oh, no," the man is saying. "We'll just watch the kids slide down. We're too old for stuff like this."

Ruth and I exchange amused glances. "Maybe I shouldn't tell them," she mutters quietly in my direction. In a normal voice, she says to the couple, "I'm sure they'll enjoy themselves."

We chuckle all the way back to the car.

"Do you think they ever noticed that we're not here with any children?" I say as we drive toward our hiking spot.

"I suppose they thought we just came by to cheer. Like the spectators at a downhill ski race. We should have brought along cow bells to ring as people approached the finish line."

Picturing a scene from the Winter Olympics, I nod. "We could suggest that to the company that runs this facility. They could rent out bells. Hire a sports commentator to describe each inner tube run over a loudspeaker."

"Have a cameraman and interviewer at the bottom to ask sledders about their strategy and how they trained for the event."

"And run Budweiser Clydesdale commercials between contestants."

Neither of us says anything for a minute, having pretty much run that idea into the ground. When we change into our hiking boots before setting out, we look at each other and simultaneously say, "Give out gold medals!"

It feels marvelous to enjoy a brief respite from stress and worries, to enjoy being playful and silly again.

***

"Have you talked with Adam yet?" Lacey's husband would have arrived home around dinnertime yesterday, and she told me he didn't have to work today or over the weekend. I'm hoping she's disclosed her secret to him already, so they'll have several days where they can focus on each other and not on work. Remembering how Carol and Nick were inseparable in the days immediately following their reunion, I imagine Lacey and Adam may feel the need to remain physically close as they face this frightening challenge.

"Yes, right after breakfast this morning. I wanted us both to be as rested as possible before I sprang it on him." She blows out a long puff of air. "You were right. I should have told him when I first found out. I think he's a little pissed off at me, but mostly he's been extremely comforting. I'm feeling more encouraged about that ninety percent and up survival rate."

"That-a girl. I don't know if keeping a positive attitude can actually cure cancer, but it certainly can help you focus on enjoying each day rather than letting the bad stuff grab all your attention." I could provide concrete examples from my own life, but she doesn't need to hear those stories right now.

"Good point. Adam said something similar. Although," she says with a half-hearted chuckle, "I'm still working on how to find enjoyment when I think I'm about to throw up."

"Oh, dear. Is that from your treatments?" Poor Lacey. I'd hoped she'd avoid side effects beyond the fatigue she exhibited earlier.

"Yeah, but they've given me something to take and it seems to be helping. Anyway, I'm hanging in there and it does feel good to have you and Em and Adam to support me. I can't believe I thought I'd be able to keep my cancer a secret once I started chemo-radiation."

"We're your team, Lacey. Don't ever hesitate to reach out to the people who love you."

"And who I love."

We chat about a few other topics – how Adam's nursing conference went, Em's new ultra-light backpacking tent she earned as a bonus from the outdoor recreation company she works for, and the weekend getaway she and Adam are planning following her final therapy appointment. "Hopefully I won't sleep through the entire weekend," she says, "but Adam says that's okay. If I'm too tired to take a walk through the town of Aspen, we'll just spend the weekend snuggled up in front of the fireplace and look out the window at the views."

I haven't had a lot of opportunities to get to know Adam

yet, but the more I learn about him, the more convinced I am that he's the perfect match for my daughter.

After we sign off, I feel a gentle wave of calmness flow through my body. Adam's reassurances have had an effect on me as well. We won't know for a while how successful Lacey's treatments will be, but I promise myself to stay as positive as possible.

Chapter 26

"I know this is crazy, but I can't stop thinking about that missing woman," I say, as Ruth snags a triple word score and pulls way ahead of me in our Scrabble game.

"I couldn't decide if you were distracted or just letting me win," she says with a smirk. "I assume you haven't heard anything more from the detective."

"Nothing." I rearrange my tiles on their tray and study the board. I could get rid of two of my three "E" tiles with "eel", or add "R" to the end of "bake." Either way, I'll still be behind. I go with "baker". Ruth lifts an eyebrow, surprised that I'm not building long words like I usually do.

"So, you still think the Zakarians are the people in the photos?" I ask. Ruth didn't seem fazed by the shaved goatee or the changes in the woman's appearance over time, but I'm still on the fence.

Ruth nods, focusing on the game until she decides on a move. "I guess all that really matters is what the cops think. I would hope they'd at least re-visit that woman's disappearance in case she really was on our trail instead of that other one."

This is going to sound nuts, but I know Ruth won't judge me harshly. "What do you think about going back and hiking up there again?"

"The Sidestep Trail?"

"Yes. And I'm curious to check out the Little Brook trail, too, where Aurora's car was found. The two trailheads aren't terribly far apart – maybe 30 miles? I don't want to *hike* Little Brook," I add, "just take a look at the trailhead and parking."

"Any particular reason why you want to go there?" Ruth asks just as the cat decides to leap into her lap and then up on the table, where she plops down in the middle of the game board and mews, asking for attention. "Oh, Charli. We're in the middle of a game."

Laughing, I concede victory to Ruth. "In answer to your question, I'm afraid it's just morbid curiosity."

Ruth's eyebrows knit and her mouth turns down. "I know it's very likely she's dead after all this time, but I keep hoping there's some other answer. Maybe she wanted out of that relationship and chose to disappear." She's rubbing the cat's cheek and the animal is purring loudly.

"Or she actually got lost and nobody's ever found any trace of her."

Ruth shudders, likely revisiting her own fears when Carol couldn't be located. I can't fathom what Aurora's parents must have gone through, having their daughter go missing like that. What they are still going through three years later with no answers.

"Of course, I don't have any expectations that we'll discover something the investigators and searchers never did," I say, "but I feel like I need to see the places again where those photos of Superman were taken, just to convince myself that we got at least *that* part right. And the other trailhead is pretty much along the way to Sidestep."

I'm asking a lot. Returning to southern Colorado takes us far off the route we had mapped out. We had planned to continue north, ending up near Jackson, Wyoming for much of August. We'll need to follow a different, longer route and make additional camping arrangements to head up that way.

"Okay, but we'll have to do some research on alternate places to stay," she says, and I smile.

"Actually," I say, pulling out my phone, "I've been doing a little homework. Remember that other campground about a mile down the road from where we stayed? It has sites available early next week and they look like they could accommodate our campers. It doesn't have hookups, though."

She's smiling and shaking her head. "We've gone without water and electricity before. I suppose you've also mapped out the entire rest of our itinerary."

I nod. Ruth knows me so well. "Shall I go ahead and book us for this coming Sunday and Monday nights? That'll give us all day Monday to explore." We're due to leave this area on Sunday anyway, and this new route will complicate things, but I've already done my research and I'm sure we can make this work without sacrificing too many days in Wyoming.

"Let's do it," Ruth says. "To be honest, I haven't been able to put that camera and the missing woman out of my mind either. Maybe this will give us a sense of having done all we could."

And maybe the investigators will discover something after all. I resolve to continue my online searches for new information about the case, at least until we've re-visited the spot where we found the camera. After that, I'll just have to let it all go.

***

"Now, what could they have sent me?" Ruth has just emerged from the Post Office in town with a small box in her hands. Carol had asked her last week where she could send a package and Ruth made sure the local Post Office would hold it for her if Carol addressed it "General Delivery." Obviously that worked.

She sits with the package in her lap, turning it this way and that and grinning. "Aren't you going to open it? Need a knife?" I ask.

"I'm trying to guess what it is," she says. "It's too lightweight to be a book and too small to be shoes, even with my kiddie-sized feet."

Oh, to have such tiny feet. Even her bulkiest hiking boots look adorable on her, unlike mine, which look like I'm directly responsible for Big Foot sightings.

"Maybe a bandana," she suggests. "No. It's a little heavier than that. A lightweight coffee mug?"

"Open it, already." I'm one of those people who rip open my presents, unable to restrain myself. Thank goodness there isn't wrapping paper on this, or she'd be carefully peeling off the tape so the wrap isn't damaged. I pop open the center console between our seats and dig out a tiny pocket knife so she can cut the box open.

With surgical precision, she slices the packing tape then ever so slowly lifts each cardboard flap. She extracts something about the size of her hand, swathed in bubble wrap and regards it closely.

"What is it?" I ask, refraining from snatching it out of her hand and unwrapping it.

Finally – finally! – she extracts an orange plastic object and we look at each other in surprise. It's the *SmartLoc* emergency device that Nick used to call for help and communicate with the sheriff's office. Why would they be mailing it to Ruth?

Peering back into the box, Ruth extracts a tiny instruction booklet and a folded sheet of paper, which she unfurls.

Mom,

We've decided to cancel the life insurance policies and "invest" that money in **2** of the newest *SmartLoc* instruments – **1** for each of us. They have a few more features and are smaller & lighter weight. We know you've got one of the earliest models, so we're sending you the one we're replacing. I think you'll find the interface easier to use.

Nick realized that having both of us carrying a locator gives him more peace of mind than the insurance ever did. And it makes sense financially, too. We'll make up for the cost of buying the **2** new units in less than **6** months vs. paying those high premiums.

Thanks for all your love and support, and especially for reminding me to focus on all the blessings in our relationship when Nick and I were going through that rough patch. Your guidance helped me stay positive when I was lost.

Stay safe! Have fun!

Love & hugs,
Carol & Nick

P.S. Does Ellie have a locator? If not, maybe you can give her your old one.

"How cool!" she says, flipping through the user manual. "Would you like my old *SmartLoc*, dear? You've seen how I've been able to pair it with my phone to customize messages on the fly."

Actually, I've been thinking of upgrading, since my locator device only lets me pre-program a few messages which correspond to buttons on the unit. I can't receive any responses, so it's far more limited than what Ruth is offering me. If Carol had been carrying their locator device, she could have not only transmitted her exact location, but could have held a text conversation with Nick when she first realized she couldn't get back to the main trail. And with rescuers, explaining her situation and learning what was happening to aid her. It's easy to imagine a situation where that extra communication could be life-saving. I gratefully accept her offer.

She calls her daughter to thank her. Once I realize that their conversation may go on for a while, I step back out of the car and settle on a nearby park bench to touch base with my own daughter. She sounds a bit more upbeat than she did when we spoke a couple of days ago.

"Taking it one day at a time," she says. "I'm halfway through my treatments!"

"How's the nausea?" I ask.

She snickers. "Not so bad – I've got medical marijuana for that and to help my appetite. It's not the kind that makes me high, though. So, I've traded nausea for other delights like having to pee constantly and diarrhea. More over-the-counter drugs, but it's too early to say how they'll do."

"Oh, dear. I hope you get some relief."

"And then there's hair loss."

At least that one shouldn't be as uncomfortable – just disconcerting. "Do you plan to shave your head?" I ask.

She laughs. "That's not where I'm losing hair."

As the saying goes, sometimes you have to laugh to keep from crying.

Chapter 27

When we reach the wildflower meadow along the Sidestep Trail, I pull up the photo from the mystery camera that we thought was taken from somewhere along here. I proceed slowly, checking for a perspective that matches the display on my phone. "Right about here," I say, handing it to Ruth so she can compare the skyline and other features.

"It matches perfectly," she says, "although they seemed to have more colorful blooms three years ago."

I feel relieved. There's no longer any doubt in my mind that the older photo was taken from this spot, so at least we weren't just letting our imaginations run wild in that respect. Of course, there are still the other possible glitches in our conclusion that Superman and Lois Lane in the photos are actually Blake and Aurora Zakarian, or if they simply resemble them. Or that the date stored with the pictures was wrong.

My gut is still telling me that we are on the right track, even if the investigators might not think so.

We continue uphill, keeping our eyes out for the place where I spied the glint from the camera. It shouldn't be too difficult to identify. Although we smoothed out the mound of dirt I dislodged when I tried to climb up the loose slope, we were hardly meticulous about it.

It seems that more dirt and debris has tumbled down onto the trail in the last four weeks, but locating our target turns out to be a no-brainer. Someone has strung about forty feet of yellow tape parallel to the trail. Every five feet or so, the words "Restricted Area Keep Out" appear. Additional strands run up the slope at either end, marking off an area that includes the spot where the camera was partially buried in dirt.

"They took us seriously!" I say, turning to Ruth. This can't be a coincidence – somebody has been up here looking at the place I marked on the map I sent to the CBI. We high-five each other. "The cops must believe there's a reasonable chance that the people in the pictures are the Zakarians. At least there's that."

"I wonder if they found anything else?" Ruth says, scanning the slope above us. Although the area doesn't appear to be greatly disturbed, I see signs that Ruth was not the only person to walk around up there.

"Come on," she says. "I'm curious to see if there are any other places they've marked off."

Hiking onward, I'm lost in thought, wondering about Aurora and her family. If anything comes from our discovery, perhaps her parents will finally learn what happened to her. And, who knows? Maybe Blake is equally devastated. We've dreamt up a scenario where he is guilty of covering up his whereabouts the day she disappeared, but what if there's another explanation?

Much farther along the trail, we come across another closed-off area, this time on the gradual slope heading downhill. It's considerably larger than the first section. Studying my map, I postulate that we're almost directly above the other search site. If the camera was lost along the trail and eventually tumbled down to where we found it, that spot would likely have been within this marked-off region. There appears to have been considerable activity on the slope below us. We spot a number of flagged stakes stuck in the ground in the area we can easily see, and the grasses and other small plants appear to be trampled. Trees and bushes block our view of lower portions of the slope, but I think I see one more flag at the edge of the more vegetated area.

"What do you think the stakes mean?" I ask. "Are they marking off areas they've already searched, or did they find something there?"

"I have no idea, but whatever they're for, it certainly looks like the searchers have been busy."

We watch for other signs that the police or search party have been at work further up the trail, but don't discover any additional tape or flags. Taking a break at the overlook, again I compare the photo of Blake Zakarian with the view we're enjoying. No question – this is the right spot.

"I suppose a lot of the people working with the police on this search are from a SAR team in this area," Ruth says as we gaze at the view while eating our lunches. "Before Carol's ordeal, I hadn't given much thought to what those people do. It's impressive. And they're volunteers!" She gestures with her peanut butter sandwich for emphasis. "Did you hear Sheriff Kat explaining that they don't charge for their service?"

I nod, my own sandwich filling sticking to the roof of my mouth.

"I'm going to send Pinnacle Search and Rescue a donation," she says.

"I'd like to pitch in on that, too." I'm guessing Ruth is considering a substantial gift, but I can certainly pitch in a hundred dollars, or perhaps a bit more. I qualified for Medicare this year, so my health insurance premiums went way down, and I'll start collecting Social Security next year. I'm feeling flush, relatively speaking.

That evening, sitting outside after we finish eating dinner, we're approached by a couple who introduce themselves as our camp hosts, Steve and Sheila.

"You folks look like hikers," Sheila says, although I have no idea how she determined that. ESP, maybe? When we acknowledge her correct assumption, she asks where we went today. Both raise their eyebrows when we report that we hiked up the Sidestep trail.

"They're letting people up there again? Those police and what-not are gone?" Steve asks.

I wonder how much they know about the search. "There wasn't anyone else around when we were there," I say, "but they've marked some areas beside the trail as being off limits."

Sheila nods. "We had a couple of folks here last week who wanted to hike there, but the police told them a search was underway, so they had to pick a different trail."

"They had search dogs with them," Steve adds, "but we haven't heard anything about anyone going missing." He glances around, then lowers his voice, as if there was anyone close enough to overhear him. "I think they were cadaver search dogs."

Ruth and I exchange glances. "Really?" I say, the reality of what that little camera might help reveal suddenly hitting home. Somehow, this has all felt like puzzling over a fictional murder mystery up until this moment. The reality of it all makes me feel slightly queasy.

"Yep. I'm thinking this has to do with that woman who disappeared maybe three, four years ago. She was supposed to be over on Little Brook, but somebody must have gotten that information wrong."

Sheila nods. "We've been hosting here for almost twenty years. Know the trails in the area like the back of our hands. Now, I don't know how anybody can get those two trails mixed up, but I remember the husband seemed a bit vague about why his wife headed out hiking by herself that day, when she didn't seem like someone who hikes much."

"Right," Steve says. "And how he claimed he was with his brother all day, but they drove up here to look for her when she didn't show up back home."

"But then they didn't call the police until the next morning because they thought you couldn't report a missing person for twenty-four hours, or some such nonsense."

I can tell we've struck a nerve. Aurora's disappearance was probably one of the biggest local news items ever for this relatively quiet portion of the Colorado mountains. These folks must feel like this happened in their own back yard.

"So, what's your theory?" I ask. "It sounds like you don't trust the husband's story."

They both shake their heads emphatically. "Not for a minute," Steve says. "To tell the truth, we're not sure exactly what happened to that young woman, but we are sure her husband knows and that he and his brother covered it up."

"It's always the husband," Sheila declares. Oddly, Steve doesn't object to her conclusion.

Ruth frowns and glances my way. I shake my head slightly, still regretting my earlier suspicions about Nick and Carol and the life insurance policy. She nods, which I take to mean that she still forgives me.

The couple go on for a bit longer about their feelings about the case, but it seems they have no additional details to share, so we excuse ourselves to clean up our dinner plates and check on the cat, who is inside the camper. They move on to another campsite to chat with its occupants.

"That was interesting," Ruth says. "I hadn't heard about them waiting to call the police."

"No. And it's interesting that they mentioned that Aurora didn't do much hiking. Remember, we wondered about that when most of the photos seemed to be in a town rather than out on a trail."

We finish cleaning up in silence, both contemplating what might have happened to Aurora. "I'm still puzzled about her car being found at that other trailhead," I say. "Supposing that her husband did something to her that day they were out together on the Sidestep trail. He could have hiked back down and then driven their car over to Little Brook. But then what?"

"Could they have started at Little Brook and made their way over to Sidestep?"

I shake my head. "The two trailheads are about thirty miles apart and the trails head off in nearly opposite directions. But what if he moved the car to Little Brook and someone drove him back to town?"

"Another hiker?" Ruth offers. "Maybe he claimed his car wouldn't start and caught a ride?"

That seems plausible. Yet, wouldn't the person who drove him back to Pueblo have come forward while this case was in the news? Blake Zakarian appeared at several news conferences in the days and weeks following Aurora's disappearance. Surely that good Samaritan would have recognized him and contacted authorities.

Unless they didn't recognize Zakarian on the news. Shaving off the goatee might have thrown him or her off.

No. That's too much of a stretch. A random hiker returning to their car might not have made the connection between a guy with facial hair in the parking area and the distraught, clean-shaven man on TV. Not if Zakarian wasn't doing anything to draw attention to himself. But someone in a car with him for an hour? Surely they'd realize he's the person they helped out.

"His brother," I say. "I think his brother helped him drop the car at the Little Brook parking area."

The same brother who provided his only alibi.

If we've developed this theory, surely the investigators have as well. I decide to focus my online search to Isaak Zakarian. And to see if I can find any updated news articles about the recent search along the Sidestep trail.

Chapter 28

It's been a long couple of travel days, but we're finally nearing Jackson, Wyoming and Grand Teton National Park. Yesterday was a nightmare, driving up Interstate 25 through Pueblo, Colorado Springs, Denver, and Fort Collins. Although I remember heavy traffic in Denver itself from my childhood, now it seems like the entire Front Range corridor is filled with an overwhelming number of cars and big rigs. I could have opted for a more scenic and slower route through the mountains, but I gave up on finding any last-minute campgrounds along that path.

Thankfully, today has been far quieter as we've angled our way northwest through Wyoming, through lengthy stretches of open range lands with a few scattered, tiny settlements breaking up the monotony. You know you're out in the boonies when you get excited seeing a sign declaring *Population 10615*, feeling like you're entering the big city. Gas stations! Several traffic lights! Boarded-up store-fronts – unfortunately. Fast food tacos!

I throw on my turn signal and pull over to the side of the road across from the taco place, thrilled that there's enough room here for both our vehicles and trailers. "Tacos okay with you?" I call out to Ruth as I approach her truck. She flashes a thumbs-up, rolls up her window, and hops out.

"I'm glad you spotted that," she says, stretching from side to side. "I was beginning to wonder if this town had any fast food places at all. I'm starving!"

The food is spicy, tasty, and quite messy. We're the only customers in the place. For the sake of the employees, I'm hoping that's simply because it's barely eleven in the morning and they've just opened. Last night's campground was far from ideal, with noise from the nearby interstate keeping us from sleeping well. It was little more than a large parking lot with spots marked off for RVs, packed in like sardines. But it was all I could find on such short notice in such a highly-populated portion of northern Colorado. We ate breakfast at 5:30 and were on the road by 6:15. I can hardly wait to reach our camp. Only a couple more hours of driving to go.

Sky High RV and Cabins is a short distance outside of the town of Jackson, nestled beside a small tributary that flows into the Snake River. Ruth's site is curled up among cottonwood trees, bordered by a thicket of wild roses, goldenrod, and lots of those yellow aster flowers that Michelle, back at the Denver Botanic Gardens, could surely name without hesitation.

My site is more open. What I lack in lovely vegetation is more than made up for in the views of the famous and drop-dead gorgeous Grand Teton mountains. More snow remains on these high peaks than we saw farther south in Colorado, offering an especially beautiful contrast to the blue skies above. Spectacular!

Although we're excited to actually enter the national park to access some of the hikes we have planned, with only a few hours available this afternoon, we decide to roam our campground, explore the narrow river, and drive back into town to stock up on food.

Later, after an early supper and another stroll, I decide to spend some time perusing the web for any possible updates on the Sidestep trail search. I was too frazzled from towing my camper through hours of heavy traffic last night to do anything but try to unwind by reading for a half hour before attempting to find a way to sleep to the sound of jake-brakes on the interstate.

A news search for "Sidestep trail" yields nothing. "Blake Zakarian" comes up with numerous hits, but I've seen these stories before. They're all from three years ago. I switch to "Aurora Zakarian" and then remember a trick that either Ethan or Gabe showed me – I can opt to limit the results to news from the past day or week rather than scroll through all those old stories again.

Oh my god. When I spot an article's title, "Human Remains Found," I feel like someone has just dumped ice water over my head. I click on the link and begin to read.

> **Based on a tip from a pair of hikers, searchers discovered a skull and other human remains near a trail in the mountains west of Pueblo, Colorado. The remains were found in**

A window pops up on the screen, obscuring the rest of the article. Rats – a pay wall. This news source wants me to subscribe before allowing me to read even one article.

Annoyed, I leave that tab open in my browser and go back to my original search, hoping that some other report might be available, but I find nothing that seems related. Too curious to give up, especially since Ruth and I were mentioned obliquely in the opening sentence, I bite the bullet and pony up ten bucks for a month's online access. I'll need to remember to cancel my subscription before they automatically charge me for next month.

I click the headline again and this time nothing prevents me from reading. The remains were found in a depression beside the roots of a toppled tree, covered loosely with dirt and rocks, I learn. It isn't until the third paragraph that the report mentions the old Aurora Zakarian case, with the officer being interviewed clearly insisting that the remains had not yet been identified, and that Aurora was thought to have disappeared some thirty miles away.

Tucking my laptop under my arm, I scurry over to Ruth's camper. We pore over the article, trying to extract every little morsel of information from each sentence.

"I think it's her," I say, looking at my friend for confirmation.

"But it could be anybody," she counters. I sigh, nodding in agreement. We stare at the computer screen. "But I think it's her, too," she says. "A make-shift grave in the same general vicinity as the camera? What are the odds?"

What would a body look like after three years? The article mentioned finding a small backpack and some clothing, so I'm picturing a skeleton covered with bits of fabric. Was the camera originally buried with her? If so, I'd guess the grave was partially exposed due to erosion and run-off from snow and rain. Did the distant yellow flag I spotted mark the gravesite? These thoughts give me the shivers. What if we had discovered a grave rather than just a camera?

I have another term to add to my future search efforts – "coroner." The County Coroner's office will be reporting on their findings about the body or skeleton soon, offering an official cause and manner of death, and hopefully the identity of the dead person.

"Did you ever imagine that camera might lead to solving a cold case?" Ruth asks. "I feel like Nancy Drew!"

I'd add her to my list of detectives, competent and otherwise. "Columbo," I suggest.

"Sherlock Holmes."

I grin as I add to the roll call. "Cagney and *Lacey*."

"How about just Ellie and Ruth?" she says. "I know I shouldn't be feeling excited about the prospect of solving the mystery of this young woman's disappearance, but ... it is a little exciting, isn't it? Exciting but terribly tragic."

We grow quiet for a bit, each considering what we've learned and our role in the case. Ruth breaks the silence first.

"I think we need some Ben and Jerry's."

"I like the way you think." I'm always up for ice cream, and we just loaded up on Cherry Garcia and Chubby Hubby flavors. Charli's favorite is plain vanilla, but she'll have to settle for pre-washing the dregs from our bowls. I doubt she'll object.

Chapter 29

Today's hike was spectacular, as we expected. We selected a relatively easy walk to a lesser-known lake, and were rewarded with tranquility and quiet. After topping out on a hill, we could gaze down on the ultra-blue lake, a delightful preview to our ultimate destination. The lake itself didn't disappoint. We enjoyed a relaxing lunch while sitting on a tiny, sandy beach with only a handful of other hikers in view.

With plenty of daylight left, after completing our hike we hop in the car and head over to the far more popular Jenny Lake. We're planning on tackling a couple of short hikes in this area tomorrow, but this gives us a chance to scope out our trailheads and stop by the visitor center for maps and additional ideas for adventures.

I gasp when Ruth picks up a brochure from a mountaineering guide service. "How hard is it to climb the Grand Teton?" Ruth asks a ranger behind the counter.

Ruth, are you totally nuts? Surely you're not considering trying it yourself!

The ranger – Brandon Rice, according to his nametag – smiles at her and glances down at the literature in her hand. "It's quite challenging," he says, nodding knowingly. "Not only do climbers have to gain over 7,000 feet in elevation, they need numerous technical skills as well. Rock climbing, rappelling, and – depending on the time of year and conditions – even some snow and ice climbing skills might be needed. It's definitely not something people should consider tackling without experience. Unless," Brandon says as he retrieves a sheet of paper from below the counter, "you go with a guide. Here's a list of the guiding companies that offer at least a day's worth of training, gear rental, and anything else someone might need to get to the summit." He waves the paper like a flag, then sets it aside.

Ruth frowns and reaches for the sheet, much to the surprise of the young ranger. She looks it over, nodding as if she's considering signing up for a trip.

"What's the age record for climbing the Grand Teton?" she asks. When Brandon wrinkles his forehead in puzzlement, she clarifies. "How old was the oldest person to climb it?"

"Oh." Brandon is looking more concerned by the minute. "Actually, we believe the legendary climber, Paul Petzoldt, still holds that record. He climbed it numerous times, including at age 86. Of course, Petzoldt was one of the top mountaineers in the world."

"Hmm. Eighty-six." Ruth hands the list of guiding companies back to the ranger. "I suppose I'd better wait and come back next year, then."

We leave poor Ranger Brandon Rice with his mouth hanging open in shock.

"Ruth – you aren't seriously considering coming back here to climb the Grand Teton, are you?"

She punches me in the arm playfully. "Of course not, dear. I just wanted that young man to realize that some elderly mountain climber may show up some day who really can beat the age record." She pauses and gazes up at the towering peaks. "I'd love to talk to somebody who's climbed it, though. How about we go over to the trailhead and see if we can spot a group coming out from the climb? If they're carrying huge backpacks and ropes and helmets and other climbing gear, they should be easy to identify."

That sounds safe enough. We locate the correct trail on our detailed map of the Jenny Lake area and make the short drive, then walk a short distance up the trail until we find an old toppled tree trunk that looks like a good place to sit and watch hikers coming and going.

It isn't long before we hone in on a likely group heading down the trail. The guy in the lead is toting an enormous load, but is marching along with a spring in his step, turning around now and then to check on the people behind him. I'm guessing he's a guide. He steps aside, motioning for the next two hikers to continue while he waits on the stragglers.

Ruth waves down the pair who reach us first – a man and woman, each carrying impressive backpacks, themselves. "Did you just climb the Grand Teton?" she asks.

"We sure did," the woman answers, beaming with joy at their accomplishment. "I've been wanting to climb *The Grand* for years, and we made it!" She and her companion slap each other's hands enthusiastically.

"You did it, babe," he says. Turning to us again, he explains that he climbed it several years ago, using a different route, but he wanted to share another ascent with his wife, who is just getting into mountaineering.

"Would you mind if I got a photo with the two of you?" Ruth asks. "I don't imagine I'll be climbing *The Grand* anytime soon, but it would be a kick to have a picture of me with some people who did."

I love how she's already latched onto their jargon – *The Grand.*

By this time, the rest of their group has caught up. One guy looks totally wiped out and he takes this opportunity to unbuckle his large pack and let it slam to the ground. The man we guessed is their guide removes his pack as well, then drapes the climbing rope over Ruth's shoulder and sets his helmet atop her head. The loops of the rope hang down to her knees. "There. Now you look like you're part of the group," he says as he positions himself to take a photo with Ruth's phone. She looks ecstatic as she poses with the first couple, then with the entire group – sans the exhausted guy who is sprawled on the ground, looking like he may need to be carried the rest of the way.

"Get in here, too," the guide tells me, and the climbers load me up with additional gear. Finally, after taking several shots of just Ruth and myself using both our phones, they help the weary man to his feet, retrieve their items, shoulder their loads, and continue down the trail. We tag along, enjoying listening to their stories about their great adventure as we hike the short distance back to the parking lot.

"That was fun," Ruth says as we watch the group depart in a van.

"Probably a lot more fun than actually doing the climb."

As I drive us back to our campground, her attention is glued to the window, marveling at the mountain range behind us. "Maybe I'll come back the summer *after* next," she says. "I'll be 87, so I could set a new age record."

I wouldn't put it past her.

Chapter 30

"Ruth! You've got to see this!"

I've just dashed out of my camper, laptop in hand. Charli is dumped off her lap as she rises swiftly from her chair and meets me at the picnic table, where I deposit my computer, screen open to a live video of a press conference.

"... are searching for Blake Zakarian, who left his home on Wednesday when it was announced that human remains had been found. His girlfriend, neighbors, family, and co-workers claim that he has not been seen since.

"Again, the remains have been positively identified as those of Aurora Esposito Zakarian. The county pathologist report states that the cause of death was blunt trauma to the head and the manner of death was homicide.

"The parents of the deceased, Sam and Lissa Esposito, will issue a statement later today. We are asking for the public's help in locating Blake Zakarian. If you know anything about his whereabouts, call the number listed on the screen. A reward of $10,000 is being offered for information leading to his arrest."

The video ends, and we stare in silence at the screen. "Oh, my," Ruth whispers. "He killed her."

"We were right." Of course, we're both fully aware that an arrest warrant doesn't prove that they're after the right person, but let's be real. He lied, he ran, and there was that darn life insurance policy he took out on her that he hasn't been able to collect on since he couldn't – *wouldn't* – prove that she was dead. How's that for a Catch-22?

Within the hour, dozens of new articles pop up in my web search, providing more background on the crime and plenty of speculation on what really transpired on the last day of Aurora's life. There's a strong implication that Blake's brother, Isaak, lied to police, helping Blake with his cover-up story and certainly with his alibi. Rumors soon explode on social media, blaming the disappearance of several other women across the U.S. on the Zakarian brothers. Claiming that Aurora had actually attacked her husband first, and that he killed her in self-defense. Postulating that Blake was part of a cult that required him to sacrifice his wife.

And those weren't even the wackiest of the theories. I shut down my social networks, realizing I'll learn nothing there.

Today was planned to be a rest day, spent reading, running a load of laundry, meandering over to the river to listen to its calming sounds, and letting all the stress of the past weeks drain away. Instead, we're both feeling wound up and in need of a physical outlet. I'm not ready for another hike, but I feel the need to do *something*.

"Back in the day," Ruth muses, "we could have had sex with our husbands, but since that's not an option..."

"Ruth!" I can feel myself blushing. I can't believe she said that.

Yes I can.

She winks and giggles. "Another possibility is to try to learn to play pickleball. There's a court over near the children's playground, and they have free rackets and balls to borrow at the office."

"Have you ever played?"

"Once," she says as she puts Charli back inside the trailer. "Valerie showed me the basics last time I visited her. It was fun. Not nearly as strenuous as tennis."

"That's good, because I suck at tennis. Or I did when I took beginning lessons when I was fourteen."

Laughing, she says, "It's slower, uses a smaller court, and we don't even have to keep score. Just whack the ball around and imagine it's that horrible man."

Since she put it that way...

Once we're ready to start, Ruth lobs the pickleball my way. My long-ago tennis experience, pathetic as it was, kicks in as I step back to swat the ball with my racket, but it barely bounces, so I miss by a mile. "Oops. Let me try again."

It takes three more attempts before I get a feel for what will happen when the ball hits the ground. It reminds me of trying to dribble an underinflated basketball – there's not much spring to its bounce. Still, when I do manage to make contact with the ball, I'm thrilled to see it clear the net so Ruth can send it back to me. I miss again, but not by much.

Soon, we're actually celebrating the occasional rally of six or seven successful returns in a row. "Now you're getting it, Ellie! Do you want to keep score?"

I'm game. She demonstrates how to serve and explains how the scoring works, which is similar to ping-pong. This could be a new *thing* for me! I played a pretty mean table tennis game back in seventh grade.

We start off fairly evenly matched, tied at two points each. But then Ruth's competitive spirit clearly kicks in – she's been sandbagging me, lobbing easy shots directly to me. Now she's running me around the court with precision, scoring point after point as I pant and pant.

"Time out!" I huff, and plop down on a bench by the fence. She trots over to join me. "I thought you'd only played this once before," I say as I dab my forehead with a tissue.

"That's true," she says, "just that one time with my younger daughter." She pats my arm. "I'm sorry, dear. I got carried away, didn't I? It seems that we woke up my old tournament spirit. Did I ever tell you that I was on my college tennis team?"

I shake my head before closing my eyes and leaning my head back against the fence. "I think you forgot to mention that."

We agree to forget about keeping score and go back to hitting the easiest possible shots to each other. When I announce that my legs have turned wobbly, we both take a turn smashing each of the balls as hard as possible across the full length of the court, in remembrance of that poor young woman who died somewhere along the Sidestep Trail.

After I shower, despite promising myself that I wouldn't immerse myself in reading about the case again, I dive in. The Espositos, Aurora's parents, read a statement to the press praising the police for re-opening the case and "finally seeking justice for the terrible crime that took our daughter from us." It's heartbreaking, but not nearly as overwhelming as a video from three years ago where Sam Esposito pleads for information about their missing child as tears stream down Lissa's face. In today's report, I sense more anger than sorrow in their faces. For three years, they've been insisting that their daughter's husband was involved in her disappearance. The authorities seemed to agree, but nobody could pull together enough evidence to charge him. Until now.

Except they still have to locate him.

***

Lacey sounds more like herself on the phone today – stronger and more upbeat. When I comment to that effect, she fills me in on what's changed.

"I've joined a group they told me about at the cancer treatment center," she explains. "I really didn't want to go to support meetings where we all sit around in a circle and share our experiences with cancer. But this is different. We go out twice a week and hike on some of the trails in the foothills just west of town."

That sounds great, but I'm having trouble reconciling my experience with her three weeks ago, where she became exhausted while walking around Denver Botanic Gardens versus her hiking two times a week.

"The side effects of your treatments must have subsided. That's good news!"

"Actually, the first time I went out with them, I felt like curling up in the fetal position and having someone carry me back to the car. But the other women encouraged me to take breaks and keep trying. And trying. I almost didn't go out with them a second time, but this one lady, Olivia, called me and insisted on picking me up to go to the trailhead. So I did, and I felt better that time. I only thought I might toss my cookies once!"

"That's amazing. So, you've kept going out with them?"

"Yes! They've been so helpful and I've made some new friends. The group is supportive and kind of cheeky and sassy. We call ourselves *Women, Trails, and Fun*. Or WTF for short."

We share a laugh at the acronym. "I never would have guessed that pushing yourself to exercise *more* would help your fatigue." But I'm thrilled that it sounds like it's working for her.

"WTF was started by a woman with metastasized breast cancer who had been training for a marathon when she was diagnosed. She started chemo, but kept training and ran the race. Her time was slower than her previous races, but she crossed that finish line. Her doctors were amazed that she stayed so active and that her cancer went into remission."

Wouldn't that be wonderful if Lacey gets the same good news once she completes her treatment! "She must be quite inspiring to hike with."

Lacey is quiet for a moment. "Actually, she died several years ago. Her cancer came back. But, Ellie, the doctors only gave her about a year to live initially. She survived and *thrived* for a decade. Up until the final month, she was still out hiking and skiing and running and living the life she loved. That's what I want. No matter what I find out from the scans once my chemo-radiation is finished, I'm going to live my life doing the things I love and spending time with the people I love."

I try to respond, but can't get any words out. My tears are flowing, but I'm smiling, hearing the strength and positivity in her words.

"Oh, and did I tell you? Adam and I have decided to start hiking together once a week. I've taken him to the trails I've done with WTF, and I think that's been really good for him, too. You know how stressful these past few years have been for healthcare workers. With that, plus dealing with my cancer, he needs an outlet as much as I do. And we're really enjoying our special time together."

I swallow and dab at my tears. "That's wonderful news, Lacey."

"Next time we get together, maybe we can go for a hike. I can't promise I can keep up with you and Ruth, but if you don't mind having a newbie along..."

"Mind? I'm thrilled with the idea. Think about some dates that might work for you and let me know. We'll make it happen."

How did I get so lucky to have a daughter like Lacey? If her parents were still alive, I'd call them up right now to thank them for their positive influence on her. I'll do my best to live up to their example.

Chapter 31

"What do you think they want to talk to us about?" I ask Ruth. Carol and Nick have been back home in San Diego for about three weeks now. Ruth has talked with them by phone several times, once on speakerphone so all of us could be in on the conversation, but Carol had insisted that today's visit be a video conference call.

"No idea," Ruth says, "but she included a long string of smiling emojis after her text message, so I'm expecting they have good news to share.

I grin at her use of the term *emoji*. Grandson Gabe got after her for still calling them *smiley faces*, and she loves to keep up with "the younger generation" and their jargon. I imagine that my granddaughter, at age 22 may not consider Gabe, who is in his mid-thirties, to be part of her "younger generation," but thirty-something certainly sounds like a younger generation to me.

We set up my laptop for our call. I position it on my picnic table so the impressive view from my campsite will appear in the background. Charli settles next to the computer in her "bread loaf pose," front paws tucked beneath her, tail wrapped tightly around her body. When we connect to the call, Nick and Carol are both grinning broadly. Ruth wriggles in excited anticipation of whatever they're planning on telling us.

"You're probably wondering why I called you all here today," Carol says, trying to keep a straight face as she offers up that old trope. She and Nick grin at each other and he mouths, "Go ahead."

"Tell us, already," Ruth says. "You both look like the cat that ate the canary."

"Ew, Mom."

"Stop with the teasing. You've got news, so come on – tell us!" Ruth leans closer to the screen.

"All right," Carol says, now smiling broadly. "So, we've been talking a lot about where we want to be in five years—"

Nick pipes in, "Retired!"

She nudges him playfully. "Right," she says. "And places we'd like to visit and how we'd like to see more of our kids and you guys."

"Carol's 'adventure' really changed our perspective on things. We have all these dreams of what our lives will look like once we retire, but nobody really knows what things will look like in five years. Or even tomorrow. Something could happen to our health or, god forbid, one of us could die."

Ruth is sitting back again and nodding slightly.

"Anyway," Carol continues, "we're taking steps toward semi-retiring in the very near future. I just gave my two week notice at work, and they've agreed to use me part-time as an independent contractor. Nick talked to his boss, and he'll be cutting back to thirty hours a week – three 10-hour days. And we can both still work remotely, like we have since the pandemic began."

"That's wonderful news!" Ruth says, beaming. I congratulate them on what is clearly a joyous change to their plans.

"But wait – there's more!" Carol says.

Nick picks up the conversation. "I'll be fully vested in my

401(k) in one more year and we'll both qualify to take Social Security within the next two years. We'll wait to see if we want to do that or not, but that takes some pressure off for retiring early."

Now it's Carol who is wriggling in her seat with excitement. "And here's the really big news: we're looking at downsizing and moving to western Colorado or somewhere in Utah or possibly northern Arizona or New Mexico. Obviously, we've got a lot of homework to do, but there are lots of places where housing prices are a fraction of what we're seeing here in San Diego, and we know we love that region."

"And we *should* downsize," Nick adds. "We bought this place while both boys were still in high school. We think we'll be able to buy something smaller in a more affordable market and pocket close to half a million dollars."

I wonder if that's part of why he was willing to cancel out that life insurance policy. No matter the reason, they both seem so much happier and in sync than before Carol got lost. It's wonderful to see them so upbeat again. And maybe we'll get to see a lot more of them in the future – that would be delightful.

"I'm so glad for you," I say. "It sounds like things are working out really well."

"Better than we imagined. The most important thing is that we've realized that we should prioritize living our dreams together *now* and not put things off until some later date. We can't quite swing full retirement yet, but this gives us more quality time together, which is our primary goal."

I tell them about my daughter embracing Women, Trails, and Fun, and how much her change of perspective seems to be lifting her spirits and drawing her family closer together.

"WTF!" Carol says. "Yes! That's exactly what Nick and I have been talking about. Quality of life, not assuming you have forever to do the things you enjoy and to be with the people you love. WTF! I'm going to think of those women getting out hiking and having fun every time I see that acronym."

"WTF!" We echo it in a chorus, fist-pumping and high-fiving.

"Willing ... To ... Flourish!" Nick says.

Carol comes up with "Winning The Future" and I offer "Wonderful Times Forever."

We all turn to Ruth. "Okay, Mom. Whatcha got for us? WTF."

Her eyes scan rapidly from side to side as she ponders her contribution. "Wild for This Family!" she announces. "Is it all right to have that extra preposition in there? I couldn't think of a 'W' synonym for Adoring."

"Ding, ding, ding," Carol says. "The judges accept that answer. It's a four-way tie for first place. Congratulations, everyone."

"Do we all get a prize?" Nick asks, just as Charli decides she needs attention and stands on the laptop keyboard facing Ruth and me, tail held tall.

"Uh, that wasn't what we had in mind," Carol quips.

Ruth immediately picks up the cat and rotates her 180° so she's facing the camera. "Charli, that's really not your good side. Let's show Carol and Nick your pretty face instead."

"WTF!" Carol says. "Whirl That Feline!"

***

I can't believe I agreed to play pickleball doubles with the couple we met at camp, Charlene and Peg. We struck up a conversation with them when we spotted them on their electric bikes, circling the loops of the campground while we walked in the opposite direction. Someone mentioned the pickleball courts and they suggested we get together to play today. Although I'm the youngest of our four competitors, I'm most definitely the one with the least experience. I knew we were in trouble when Charlene and Peg showed up with their own paddles, which they retrieved from an attractive zipped case, and a mesh bag filled with balls. Ruth never flinched.

Playing with Ruth on my side is certainly less strenuous than what we did my first time out. I have only half the area to cover, and Ruth has me focus on longer shots that usually have bounced, while she tackles plays closer to the net that require a quicker response. Miraculously, we keep the score tight until the very end, when the other ladies pull ahead for the win.

We continue playing and our new friends extend their winning streak, always by a thin margin. Ruth is the one who returns about 75% of their volleys, but I manage a few shots that make me feel proud of myself.

After our third game, I beg to be excused and just be a spectator. Ruth graciously joins me on the bench as Peg and Charlene take on each other. It doesn't take a pickleball expert to realize that they've been holding back and letting us score points – they're astonishingly adept at this sport. Ruth and I exchange glances. "Well, that puts things in perspective," she says. "I think we're going to need a lot more practice."

"Yeah, but I'll bet neither of them is planning on climbing *The Grand* when they're 87."

After we all return to our respective campsites, I notice that I've missed a text message from Ethan that he sent to both Ruth and myself.

> **Grammas – did you see this update about the camera people? The plot thickens!**

I click on the link he's included and it brings up a news article. Shoot – the font is too small to read, but if I enlarge it, I can only see about five words in a sentence at a time. Too frustrating. Instead, I pull up the link using my laptop's browser history so I can read it properly.

Wow – they're still searching for Blake Zakarian, but now, instead of referring to him as a *person of interest*, the police are seeking to arrest him on first degree murder charges. It says that his brother, Isaak, is now "cooperating" with authorities as part of a plea-bargaining agreement with the District Attorney's office on "various charges." The brother has recanted his statements to police that Blake was with him on the day Aurora disappeared and has admitted to helping him relocate Aurora's car so that it would appear that she was on the Little Brook trail.

Grabbing my computer to hurry over to Ruth's, I find her heading my way. "You've seen the article?" she says. "I read the first paragraph but it was too hard to see the whole thing on my phone."

We step back inside my place and I give her a minute to read the rest of the story.

"Oh, my," she says. "That poor girl. And her family! I hope they find that monster and lock him up for life."

"So, the brother finally grows a conscience. Or they had him over a barrel for lying to police and covering up a major crime."

Ruth ponders this a moment. "I imagine they suspected him of lying right from the beginning. Remember? We read something about the police believing Blake Zakarian was involved in Aurora's disappearance, so they must have figured Isaak was providing a false alibi. They just couldn't find enough evidence that they thought would hold up in court."

"That's a good point. I wonder what changed once her body was found. Maybe they also found something that more clearly connected Blake to her murder?"

Ruth raises her eyebrows and tilts her head to one side,

challenging me to answer my own question. "Of course – it was the camera!"

Faced with the police knowing he had lied about his brother's whereabouts, did Isaak see their house of cards crumbling and realize that he might also be charged as an accessory to murder? Perhaps.

How long can that scumbag hide from police? I pray they'll find him soon and that Sam & Lissa Esposito get the small comfort of seeing him answer for his loathsome crime.

Chapter 32

This is a day I've been preparing for with great anticipation as well as trepidation. Lacey's radiation and chemo treatments are finally finished and she's awaiting her test results. Not wanting to be out of cell phone range when she calls, I've remained in camp, attempting to make progress on the novel I've been reading. I doubt I'll ever make it to the next chapter until I've heard from her.

Ruth offered to stick around to keep me company, but I insisted that she go ahead and hike without me. We both know she was actually offering to be here for support in case the news is bad. If that turns out to be the case, I think I'll need a little time alone to process it. *Then* I'll let Ruth help me gather my strength so I can offer that support to Lacey, Adam, and Em.

Think positive. Think positive.

When the start time for her appointment arrives, I can no longer sit still. I clutch my phone in my hand and start to walk the campground roads, checking the display constantly to reassure myself that I still have cell coverage and that the ring volume is on high and that it is also set to vibrate. How much longer until she has an answer? *Is Adam there with her?* Of course he would be. *Will they call Em first with the results?* Most likely.

To try to settle my nerves, I play a mental game of promising myself I won't check the time for at least fifteen minutes. I walk over to the stream and toss small twigs in the flow, seeing how far they drift before getting caught up in grasses and other vegetation growing up through the slow, shallow waters. A movement catches my attention and I spot a bull elk standing in the meadow on the far side of the tributary, probably a hundred feet from me. His multi-pronged antlers look formidable, but his powerful neck muscles seem up to the task of carrying all that weight. We stare at each other for a moment, then he turns his head and looks elsewhere. Jutting his head forward, he emits the classic bugling sound, which seems remarkably high-pitched coming from such a large animal. I'm surprised to encounter an elk in rut this early – I had always thought they only bugle in September, which is still a few weeks away. If the early bird gets the worm, maybe the early bull elk gets the elk harem.

I nearly drop my phone when it starts playing "Mother and Child Reunion" – my ringtone for my daughter. "Lacey," I practically shout. "Any news?"

"Hi Ellie. Yes, I have good news."

Then why am I hearing some hesitation in her voice?

"It's gone into remission."

There's still something she isn't saying, but I decide to forge ahead. "That's wonderful, Lacey. Just what we were hoping for! You and Adam will have a lot to celebrate this weekend in Aspen."

Now she lightens up. "We certainly will. When we first planned it, I didn't expect to be able to enjoy walking around and really enjoying the surroundings, but with the hiking we've been doing, there'll be much more that we'll be able to experience."

"I'll bet you're relieved to be finished with all the drugs and radiation treatments. The side effects should start to fade now, right?" We talked about that when she first started reacting to the therapy.

"Probably. But Ellie, you do understand that being in remission isn't the same as being cured? The therapy reduced the amount of cancer and it hasn't spread since my treatments began, but it's still there. I'll be having regular follow-up tests and if it takes off again, they'll start me on some medication that's supposed to keep it under control. But I'm not *cured*."

That's where her hesitation was coming from. "Still, remission is a good result. I've been reading some articles about cervical cancer, by the way. Some doctors won't use the term 'cured' even if no cancer cells can be detected. So don't feel disheartened. Consider this a success. Keep on Walking those Trails and having Fun. WTF!"

She chuckles. "WTF! You're right. If I focus on the positive, life is a lot more fun. Thanks, Ellie."

She signs off, explaining that she still needs to talk to Adam's parents, who are already on a call with him, sharing their news. I congratulate her again, and wish them both a wonderful weekend.

Like Lacey, I was hoping the doctors would declare her totally free from cancer. But *remission* is what we're faced with, so we'll have to deal with that one day at a time and see what the future brings.

Chapter 33

Our daily lives relax back into a comfortable pattern. Ruth and I hike three or four days each week, some of them long and strenuous, but interspersed with gentle outings. We've discovered a few favorite trails in the Jackson area, and love repeating them, sometimes with new friends we've made at the campground. Peg and Charlene moved on to their next destination last week, but not before coaching both of us in pickleball and letting us win a game. They offered to let us try out their e-bikes – Ruth accepted without hesitation, but they couldn't coax me into riding around the campground.

On our rest days, we both often read, run errands, catch up on phone calls to family and friends, and take Charli on short outings in her kitty pack. August is nearly over, as is our time here by Grand Teton National Park. We'll be heading north to visit Yellowstone soon, spending three weeks in total, but at multiple campgrounds since we weren't able to reserve anything for the entire period. From there, we'll start working our way back to northern Arizona by October, and then on to the southern Arizona desert region for the cooler months.

We had pretty much given up on hearing anything new on the manhunt for Blake Zakarian when I happen to notice a headline in my news feed from a local paper in southern Colorado.

Human Remains Found in Canyonlands
Identified as Murder Suspect

Could it be?

The opening paragraph answers my question.

"Dental records confirmed that human remains found by a pair of backpackers in a remote area of Canyonlands National Park were those of Blake Zakarian, a suspect in the murder of his wife, Aurora Zakarian. According to his autopsy report, his death was ruled a suicide. He died from a gunshot wound to the head."

I have to wait a day to discover a small piece from that same newspaper that mentions the case again. A photo of Aurora's parents, Sam and Lissa Esposito, accompanied by a young man and woman – her brother and sister, I learn from the caption – appears with a formal statement from the family, thanking the police, the sheriff's department, the CBI, and the search teams who located Aurora's grave, for their support and diligence in investigating this case over more than three years. I wonder how the family felt during the long period when no progress was made in bringing Aurora's killer to justice. Perhaps their frustration was aimed more at the system that declined to charge the man rather than the investigators who sought in vain to nail down enough evidence against him.

I click on a video that accompanies the article. Sam Esposito reads the statement aloud as his family looks on. Then, the young woman, whose large brown eyes are remarkably similar to her late sister's, takes the microphone from her father's trembling hands.

"My name is Antonia Esposito Trujillo and Aurora was my little sister," she says, looking directly into the camera. "About 2,000 women in this country are killed by their husband or partner each year. Most of these cases get very little attention. My sister was more than just a statistic. She was a loving auntie to my two girls and to Ricardo's son," she says, indicating her brother. "She was a generous soul who volunteered at the local food pantry. She was a talented singer who led the children's choir at our church. She was a valued employee at an oral surgeon's office, scheduling appointments and helping nervous patients relax before their procedures."

She takes a deep, steadying breath. "She was taken from us far too soon, but I wanted people to know a little bit about my sister. Don't forget her. We never will."

Tears flow down my face as I watch Antonia hand the microphone to her brother.

"Just one final thing," he says. "We're grateful to the hikers who found Aurora's camera and cared enough to try to locate its owner. Without that, we might never have learned what really happened to our sister."

Oh, my heart.

Chapter 34

What was that?

With a strong sense of déjà vu, I freeze, then step back slightly. Incredibly, there's a glint of reflected sunlight just uphill from our trail.

"What is it, dear?"

This time the slope is gentle and the shiny object is only a few easy steps away. I laugh when I retrieve it, holding it up for Ruth to see.

"Just a pretty rock." I step back onto the trail and hand it to her.

"Quartz," she says as she rotates it in her hand. "Very lovely."

Also fairly common in this area. She hands it back to me and I'm about to toss it back to the ground when she reaches out for my arm.

"Let's keep it to remember her by."

I hold the white cluster in the palm of my hand, turning it to admire the sharp angles of the crystals. There's a pretty patch of pale orange in one spot, and some of the specimen is marked with dark, narrow lines.

There are probably thousands of other bits of crystal along this trail, but each one is unique. As Aurora was.

She will not be forgotten.

ABOUT THE AUTHOR

Diane Winger is a retired software developer who loves to seek outdoor adventures, either close by her western Colorado home or farther afield, using her Aliner camper-trailer as home base. She and her husband, Charlie, enjoy hiking, rock climbing, cross-country skiing, and kayaking, and fill their evenings with reading, writing, playing Scrabble, or planning their next trip.

She is an enthusiastic volunteer in their small community, with a particular fondness for literacy-enhancing projects.

Diane and Charlie are co-authors of several guidebooks on outdoor recreation. *Ellie Dwyer's Startling Discovery* is Diane's 11th novel.

http://WingerBooks.com

Dear Reader,

I hope you enjoyed ***Ellie Dwyer's Startling Discovery***.

As an author, I thrive on feedback. You, the reader, are a major part of my inspiration to write, to explore my characters, and to try to bring them to life. So, please let me know what you liked or disliked. I'd love to hear from you. You can email me at **books@WingerBookstore.com**, or visit me on the web at **WingerBooks.com**.

Just one more thing. I would consider it a great favor if you would post a review of ***Ellie Dwyer's Startling Discovery***. Whether you loved it or hated it, or anything in between, I appreciate your feedback. Reviews can be difficult to come by. Every review can have an enormous impact on the success or failure of a book.

You can find all of my titles on my Author Page on Amazon – the link to it is **amazon.com/author/winger**. Please visit my page and, if you have time, leave a review. You can also "follow" me on Amazon or on BookBub to receive news when a new title is available.

Thank you so much for reading this book and for spending time with me.

Sincerely,
Diane Winger

Also by Diane Winger

Faces
Duplicity
Rockfall
Memories & Secrets
The Daughters' Baggage
The Abandoned Girl
No Direction Home
Ellie Dwyer's Great Escape
Ellie Dwyer's Big Mistake
Ellie Dwyer's Change of Plans
Ellie Dwyer's Startling Discovery

With Charlie Winger

Highpoint Adventures
The Essential Guide to Great Sand Dunes
    National Park & Preserve
The Trad Guide to Joshua Tree

Made in the USA
Columbia, SC
02 April 2022

58412205R00141